LOST MEMORIES AND NEW BEGINNINGS

LORANA HOOPES

To my wonderful readers who inspire me to write everyday.
To my lovely BETA readers who helped me make this the best book it could be - Deanna, Cassandra, Shari, Billie, Linda, and Dan.
To Dan, my amazing proofreader, who wordsmiths with the best of them.
To Linda who told me this character's story needed to be told.
To Molly who helped me with the hospital scenes to make them more realistic.

NOTE FROM THE AUTHOR

Thank you so much for picking up this book. I never expected to add suspenseful stories to my repertoire, but I thoroughly enjoyed Fire Games and felt like more characters in that book deserved a story. This is only the second one, but I have a whole series planned. I hope you like this book. If you do, please leave a review at your retailer. It really does make a difference because it lets people make an informed decision about books.

If you are reading this book, you also qualify for a special bonus. Simply email your receipt or the first word of chapter 10 to loranahoopes@gmail.com and I'll send you a short story of Detective Jordan Graves's side of the story "When Questions Abound." Just my way of saying thank you.

Sign up for Lorana Hoopes's newsletter and get her book, The Billionaire's Impromptu Bet, as a welcome gift. Get Started Now!

CHAPTER 1

*A*t the sound of the angry voices, she clasped her hand over her mouth to keep from making a sound. She had to get out of here, but the men were still in the room. Was this why he had been so angry when she came back? What would they do if they found her?

She faintly heard the sliding glass door to the balcony patio open. Now was her shot, and it might be the only one she had. As quickly as she could, she pushed open the door. *Don't look at them. Just grab your purse and get out of here.* But her eyes shifted to the left anyway. As if drawn by force. For a moment she froze. Long enough for the man on the patio to turn and catch sight of her. His face was shrouded in darkness, but she could feel the frosty hatred in his gaze. Her feet regained their ability to move and she bolted out of the bedroom and down the stairs.

A noise sounded behind her, but she didn't know if it was the patio door or her overactive imagination playing tricks on her. She burst out the front door and raced down the driveway knowing the men were just behind her. Her breath and the sound of her heartbeat thundered in her head. Would she make it? Frantically, she pushed the unlock button on her key fob. She wanted to turn around, but she knew looking behind her would cost precious time. When she reached the car, she yanked the door open and slid into the seat. Her fingers trembled so badly that she nearly dropped the keys as she jammed them into the ignition. As it finally slid in, she chanced a glance at the front door.

He stood there in the shadows looking as if he belonged in the darkness. As if he owned it. She jerked the car into drive and sped out of the driveway certain that he would jump in a vehicle and follow her.

Fear and anger took turns controlling her body as she drove. Tears blurred her vision, and she blinked against the dam determined to hold them in. She would not cry. She did not cry. But what was she going to do now? It was supposed to have been a simple meeting, a chance to land a new publisher for her books after the last company dropped her. Instead it had turned into something else, something nefarious feeling, and she was a witness. A witness who was never supposed to be there.

She glanced in the mirror to see if he was following her, but only darkness stared back at her. He hadn't seemed in a hurry as he stood in the front doorway, but now he knew what she drove. Would he hunt her down? Why hadn't she done better homework on him?

Disgust filled her as she thought of how she had come crawling to him. How she was willing to do nearly anything to get him to promote her. How could she have gotten involved with a man like that? Well, almost involved. Her momma sure wouldn't be proud. Heck, she wasn't proud. She had no idea how she had wandered so far down the wrong path.

Maybe it had been the move to California or the first award. After all, she'd been a poor girl growing up with only her big imagination to keep her company. Especially after her father left them. Maybe it had been the first time she saw her name on a cover. When she'd first begun writing, she'd been young and idealistic. She'd wanted to write clean romances that people could read anywhere and not be ashamed, but the publishing world was competitive. New authors were writing books every day and her work wasn't selling the way it used to. Then, after her attempt to discredit Ava McDermott had backfired, her publisher had let her go. Now, she had a stack of bills that needed to be paid and no way to do it. That was why she had gone to him.

But he'd wanted more than her books. He'd lured her here with big promises and the right words that fed her ego, but he'd really just wanted to get her into his bed. That low down, dirty…. No, she would own this. She had reached out to him. She had been the one trying to further her career. She was the one who hadn't done her homework completely. His personal life should have been in her research. Maybe then she would have known about whatever he had going on the side. Well, that wouldn't happen again. She would just have to be more careful in the future - cross all the "t"s and dot all the "i"s. If there was a future.

She wiped her finger across her cheek. A tear had escaped her eye and was trying to snake down her cheek, but she wasn't going to let it succeed. Of course, what would smeared makeup matter if he went after her? Her makeup should be the least of her worries.

Suddenly headlights flared in her rearview mirror. Bright and unforgiving, they blinded her, forcing her to throw up a hand. Oh no, had he pursued her after all? The lights grew closer and filled her mirror. Was he trying to run her off the road? Maybe it wasn't him. Maybe it was just teenagers out for a joy ride, but they were driving awfully close to her - dangerous on city streets.

She slowed down to let the vehicle pass, but it didn't. Instead, it matched her pace. These weren't teenagers then. They would have driven past her. Maybe yelled or flipped her off, but they would have passed her. Her tears dried up as fear overtook her anger and self-pity. How was she going to get out of this now? She was unfamiliar with this area and had no idea how to outrun them.

She twisted in her seat to try and get a better view of the vehicle behind her, but it was too dark and they were too close. She glanced around for her phone to call 911 but it was on her passenger seat. Just out of reach. Wait! Where was her purse? Oh no, she had left it there. Her heart sank. Now they would know for sure who she was and where she lived.

The fear grew icy talons and clawed up her insides. Were they going to run her off the road and then shoot her? Suddenly, lights flashed to her right. She had just enough time to register a large dark truck approaching and then her head was thrown into the window with the impact.

"HELP! IS THERE A DOCTOR IN HERE?"

Dr. Brody Cavanaugh looked up from his sparkling water to the doorway to see what the commotion was. A man stood in the doorway wringing his hands. Frantic fear covered his face, and his eyes shifted from one face to another as he scanned the crowd.

"There was an accident. A woman's been injured, but the guy who hit her took off. She looks bad though. Are any of you doctors?"

"I am." Brody knew Hollywood thought

this happened all the time, but he could honestly count on one hand the times someone had come running in calling for a doctor and only one had happened since he'd been in Fire Beach. He caught fellow doctor Nick Pearson's attention and pushed back from the table. His drink could wait. As could his dinner. He and Pearson fought their way through the throng of patrons and spilled out onto the street with the rest of the crowd following behind them.

The sun had set, but the streetlights illuminated the area, and down the street he could see the car – a red sports car – folded in a "C" shape. For one moment, time appeared to freeze as people assessed the situation. And then everything happened at once.

"Get the Jaws of Life," one of the firemen ordered as he sprinted towards the car. Tall and muscular, Brody thought he was the one they called Bubba. Around Brody, firemen spread out. Some ran toward the firehouse a block away to get the truck and the ambulance, and others ran with the large fireman toward the car including Cassidy.

Brody had met Cassidy a few times at the hospital when she came in with paramedic Ivy Hopkins, but it was not until he had assessed her after her abduction a few months ago that the bond between the hospital, the fire department, and the police department had begun to grow. Even though he worked in the ICU now instead of the emergency department, he had been kept in the loop of events, such as tonight's opening of her boyfriend's, Detective Jordan Graves, restaurant, Fire Dreams. However, this was probably not the opening Cassidy and Jordan had planned on or hoped for.

The firetruck and ambulance roared in a moment later, and two more large men carried the bulky machinery over to the car. Brody approached and stood to the side watching as Bubba and one of the other firemen worked the Jaws of Life to cut away the driver's door. The groaning sound of the metal snapping not only overpowered the roaring of the hydraulic tool but reminded him of nails on chalkboards, and he resisted the urge to place his hands on his ears. The red sports car was twisted in such an awkward shape that he feared the driver had been crushed in the crash.

Ivy Hopkins appeared beside him having hopped down from the ambulance. Her wide eyes were fixed to the scene. "Do you think she'll make it?" Her slender fingers pulled on the ends of her blonde hair.

"I don't know, but we'll do everything we can." Brody exchanged a glance with Nick. They both knew this driver needed a miracle.

"Her legs are pinned under the dashboard," one of the men called out as the deafening sound of the hydraulic ceased momentarily. The sudden stillness was jarring. "We need the ram."

Two other firemen hurried forward with a different tool and after a moment, the hydraulic sound filled the night again.

"Okay, we've got her free."

That was their cue. The firemen stepped aside as he, Nick, and Ivy stepped up to the car. Brody tried not to focus on the metallic scent of blood in the air or the mangled mess that was the woman's right leg as he surveyed the scene closer. The woman wore a red suit, designer from the looks of it, and red acrylic nails covered her fingertips. She was either a woman of means or one who took pride in her appearance. He leaned toward the former assumption based on the car she was driving. A Firebird wasn't the cheapest car to own or insure.

Ivy checked for a pulse and performed a

quick assessment of the woman before strapping on a neck collar. "She's breathing, but her vitals are weak." Her eyes locked with his and said more than her words did. She unfastened the seat belt and moved it away from the woman taking extra care to pull it away from her right side which had taken the brunt of the force. Then she stepped back allowing him to snake his arms under the woman's arms while Nick took the woman's legs.

The woman's face and hair were covered in blood, and Brody thought some of the cuts on her face might need stitches, but that was not his immediate concern. No, his immediate concern was her head. A large cut indicated she had hit her head against the window and her lack of response pointed to a concussion if not a possible brain injury. Plus, there was the probability of internal bleeding.

Nick appeared to share his assessment as he glanced up with grave eyes as they placed the woman on the stretcher. "Her right foot is in bad shape too."

"I'm going to call ahead and tell them what's coming," Ivy said as she caught a full glimpse of the woman.

Brody nodded as he and Nick helped the

other paramedic load the gurney into the ambulance. Ivy returned and climbed in the back with Brody as the other paramedic and Nick climbed into the cab. Brody's previous ER training kicked in and he took a closer look at the woman's feet as Ivy set up an IV. Her shoes were expensive looking red heels and though he knew she might be angry, her feet were already beginning to swell, and he couldn't wiggle the shoes enough to get them off. "Do you have scissors in here?"

Ivy handed a pair back to him and he inserted them in the side, cutting away the shoes until he could remove them from her feet.

"Is she going to lose them?" Ivy asked.

"Probably not the left one. It might be broken or sprained, but the right? I don't know, but it doesn't look good." The skin was still intact which was a good sign, but purple bruising was already starting to appear. It had been mangled badly in the crash and was twisted in an awkward angle. He just hoped that it had not been crushed. Crush injuries generally resulted in amputations, and though he knew they weren't the end of the world, no doctor liked performing them especially on someone so young. If she didn't lose it, she would probably need some reconstructive surgery on it.

The ambulance pulled to a stop, and the back doors opened. Nick and the other paramedic pulled the gurney down as Ivy and Brody climbed out after. Together they sprinted into the hospital. A wave of nostalgia hit him as the doors whooshed open.

"Female: mid-thirties, motor vehicle crash with jaws of life extrication, BP is ninety over palp, pulse is tachy and thready, O2 sats low nineties with fifteen liters on a nonrebreather.. we secured I.V. access in route - sixteen gauge in the left AC," Ivy rattled off as the doctors on shift swarmed in around them.

"She sustained a substantial head injury with loss of consciousness as well, and her legs and feet need to be addressed," Brody added. "Particularly the right side. There might be crushing involved."

"Thank you, Dr. Cavanaugh. We can take it from here," Dr. Williams said brusquely.

Brody opened his mouth to protest but then closed it. This was no longer his domain, and she was a competent doctor. In fact, she had been the one who had taken his position when he moved. He trusted her, but Brody didn't want to let her take the woman. He wanted to jump in and work on this woman himself, but he would get his chance. He'd be on shift in less than eight hours, and she would probably end up in the ICU. He could check on her then. If she made it through the night.

CHAPTER 2

*T*he woman tried to open her eyes and grimaced against the pain. "Where am I?" Her voice sounded groggy and far away, and her head throbbed. After a few tries, she managed to get her right eye open, but the left didn't seem to work.

"Fire Beach Hospital. I'm Dr. Cavanaugh. How are you feeling?"

She searched for the source of the voice and found a handsome man in a white coat at the foot of her bed. His coppery hair was combed back and his face sported a neatly trimmed beard and mustache. He held a clipboard in his hands. A doctor? Was she in a hospital?

The woman groaned and closed her eyes

as another wave of pain followed by a wave of nausea hit. When it passed and she was sure she wouldn't vomit when she opened her mouth, she answered his question. "Like I've been hit by a train." She attempted to raise her hand to touch her head but cords and pain made her lay it back down.

"Close." He nodded and gave her a small smile. "'We heard it was a black Ford truck. The police are looking for them now, but can you remember anything else?"

She tried to focus. "I was in an accident?" She felt like she should remember that, and there was this tiny spot in her brain that felt like a memory, but it was fuzzy and far away.

"You were. Banged you up pretty badly. Your left eye is swollen shut which is why you can't open it right now. You have a pretty deep contusion on your head, and your right foot was broken, but it looked a lot worse initially. Thankfully, you have no internal bleeding, but you were unconscious for a while. Can you remember anything about the accident?"

Fear. A feeling of fear crackled in the air. She remembered fear coursing through her body and bright lights. "I think someone was after me."

He raised an eyebrow as he marked something on his clipboard. "What makes you think that?"

"I don't know." Her words sounded desperate and angry in her ears. "I just feel like I was running from something, and someone was chasing me."

"Okay, we'll come back to that later." She could tell from his voice that he didn't believe her, but she knew what she felt. She didn't remember the details but the lingering caress of fear didn't dissipate.

"Let's start with something easier. Can you tell me your name?"

What kind of stupid question was that? Certainly she knew her name. It was... Suddenly her right eye shot open and her heart thundered harder in her chest. The caress of fear shifted into a full embrace that covered her body. She caught the doctor's gaze and forced the fearful words out. "I don't remember my name. Is that normal?"

His jaw tightened - just the slightest twitch near his chin - but the movement was brief, and she wondered if she had just imagined it. "It can happen in cases like this. You hit your head pretty hard, and you had a concussion which can cause some memory loss. The CT showed some swelling, so we'll continue to monitor it."

"It will come back though, won't it?" Anxiety joined the fear coursing through her body. She couldn't have lost her memory.

"I've seen patients regain some memory, depending on how severe the concussion was."

"Some memory? I can't lose any of my memory." A desperate fear ravaged her and colored her voice. What would she do if she couldn't remember her life? "You have to do something to get it back."

He chuckled softly and shook his head. "There's no trick I can do if that's what you're looking for, but it does help if you don't stress yourself out."

"Not stress myself out?" Her voice took on a sharp edge. "That's easy for you to say, but I don't even know who I am at the moment, and there are clearly people out to get me, so not stressing is not really an option."

His smile faded, and a cool expression covered his face. "I know you're scared, but I need you to stay calm."

"Wait, what about identification? Did I have a purse? I feel like I don't go anywhere without a purse." She was desperate, but maybe if she saw her name it would all come flooding back.

"I'll check with Detective Graves who is probably the one handling your case. If there was a purse, we'll get it to you. Now, why don't you relax and let me examine you?"

The woman tried to relax but her brain continued to spin. Surely someone was missing her. Was she married? Did she have kids? Her gaze traveled to her left hand, but there was no ring. Had they removed her jewelry? "Did I have anything when I came in? Any jewelry?"

"I'm not sure, but I'll check." He shined a light in her eyes. "How is the pain in your head?"

"Awful. It feels like someone's beating a gong inside my brain." She paused for a minute. Those words felt familiar as if she'd heard them before.

Dr. Cavanaugh chuckled. "Well, that's a saying I haven't heard before, so I bet you're not from around here."

She wasn't even sure where here was at the moment, but before she could ask, he continued. "How about your feet?"

She closed her eyes and tried to focus on

her feet, but there was so much pain coursing through her body that she couldn't be sure where it was coming from. "All I feel is pain. Can't you give me something for the pain?"

"I have you on an IV delivering pain medicine. I can't give you any more, but the pain will lessen as you heal. Now, can you feel this?"

She blew out a frustrated breath and concentrated on her foot. Perhaps she felt something, but she wasn't sure. "Um, maybe?" She glanced up at him. From the expression on his face, that wasn't the answer he wanted. "Is it bad?"

"It's not what I would like, but it might be that the pain you are feeling is still affecting your movement. We'll give it another few days." He continued the exam pressing gently on her stomach and her thighs before scanning both her arms. When he appeared satisfied, he stepped back.

"Do you feel up to eating? I can have Valerie bring you some food."

Eating? How could she think about eating? Her world had just been turned upside down, but he must have taken her lack of response as a yes as he continued his spiel.

"If you would like to watch TV, the

remote is here." He picked it up and waved it before setting it back beside her, "and here on the side of the bed is the call button. If you need a nurse, you hit that button. This button here you can hit if you need more medicine, but it will max out at a certain level. I'm afraid we can't take all the pain away. I'll be back to check on you before I leave for the day."

Anxiety clutched at her heart, and she heard it in her voice. "You mean you aren't going to be monitoring me directly?"

"I'm afraid I have other patients that I also have to check on, but I will look back on you before I leave."

She watched him walk out the door and tried to keep her tears in check, but the silence of the room pressed in on her. Except for the beeping of some monitor, she was alone. With no idea of who she was or when she might remember.

BRODY SIGHED as he exited the woman's room. He had expected her to be demanding from the persona he had created of her, but he hadn't expected the memory loss. While some patients did regain their memories, many didn't, and he certainly couldn't release her until at least some of her memory returned. Plus, the loss of sensation in her feet bothered him. He had seen no blackening of her skin which was hopeful - it meant her foot was still getting blood flow, but that didn't mean she would be able to walk on it again if she didn't get sensation back.

"I was hoping I would find you here."

Brody looked up to see Detective Jordan Graves and a young-looking woman striding his direction. Jordan held a mangled object in his hand. "Dr. Cavanaugh, this is my partner, Al Parker. The woman had a phone in the car," he said holding up the object, "but no wallet. Is she awake yet?"

"She is, but she doesn't remember much. Not even her name."

The woman, Al, blinked at him. "Is that normal? Will she get it back?"

Brody shrugged and picked up the next patient info sheet. "I don't know. She hit her head pretty hard and sustained a concussion, but the CT didn't show any lasting damage although it did show swelling. My guess is that she will get at least some back, but I can't give you a timeline."

"Is she able to talk? Can we ask her some questions?" Jordan pressed.

"She is capable of speaking but don't push her too hard. Rest is important for her right now, and again, I don't think she remembers much. Although she does think someone was after her."

"She does? What did she say?"

"Not much. Just that she remembered being afraid and thought someone was after her. I was about to refer her to psych for an examination."

Jordan's jaw clenched and he exchanged a glance with Al. "Hold off on that for a while, will you? She might be right. We found no brake marks on the road and our witness said the truck didn't even try to stop. My gut says this might not have been an accident, and we are determined to find out who hit her and why. Which room is she in?"

"Room six." Brody pointed behind him and watched the two detectives walk away. He felt his view of the woman shifting. She might be a bit challenging, but why would someone be after her? He found himself curious about her.

Maybe it was because he had been one of the first responders on the scene and ridden with her in the ambulance. Maybe it was because she seemed so vulnerable both with her injuries and with her memory loss. Whatever the reason, he needed to think less about the Jane Doe in room six and more about his job before he made a mistake.

CHAPTER 3

*T*he woman looked up at the knock. A man in blue jeans and a leather jacket and a younger woman in a button-down shirt stood in the doorway of her room.

"Pardon me, ma'am, but I'm Detective Graves and this is Detective Parker. Do you think we could ask you a few questions?"

The woman lifted her hand a few inches and motioned them inside. "You can try, but I don't remember much – not even my name. The doctor already asked."

A small smile pulled at the male detective's lips. "Well, no offense to Dr. Cavanaugh, but he's not a detective, so he might not have asked the right questions." He held out a broken phone. "Do you recognize this?"

The woman looked at it and an image flashed in her mind. She closed her eyes against the fear that accompanied the vision. "That's my phone, isn't it?"

"We pulled it from your car, so we believe it was your phone."

"I was going to use it, but it was on the passenger seat and I couldn't reach it, but I can't remember why I was going to use it."

"Unfortunately, it's destroyed and there was no purse or wallet inside the car that we could find. Do you know why you might have been driving without your license?"

She opened her mouth to reply but then paused. Driving without a license was illegal. Somehow, she knew that, so was he trying to trick her? "Am I in trouble, officers?"

He stared at her for a second before chuckling softly. "For driving without a license? No. You should always carry it and you can be fined for not having it, but we're not here to issue you a ticket. We're more concerned with the accident. Our witness says the black truck hit you, but we aren't sure if the accident was on purpose or not. Do you remember anything?"

Just the fear. "I don't think it was an accident. I can't remember why, but I think someone was after me. Did the witness help at all?"

The female detective stepped forward, "He wasn't able to supply us with much unfortunately, so we were hoping this phone might jog some memories."

"I wish it did, but I have nothing more."

"That's okay, it will probably come back," Detective Graves said before the ringing of his phone interrupted him. He pulled it out and turned away. "Detective Graves. Yes, sir, we are here now. Tia Sweetchild?" He glanced back at her. "Yes sir." He hung up the phone and returned to the side of her bed. "Does the name Tia Sweetchild ring a bell for you?"

"Is that me? Am I Tia?" she asked.

"The car you were driving was rented to a Tia Sweetchild so yes, we believe so. However, the address listed on the rental agreement is in California, so we're not sure what you would be doing here in Illinois."

She rolled the name around in her head. It didn't feel wrong, but she wished it zinged or something, so she could feel certain. Still, it was better than having no name. "I have no idea what I was doing here, but now that we know my name, we should be able to find out some more about me, right?"

"We'll certainly do our best," Detective Parker said. "If you remember anything else, please call us." She handed Tia a white business card.

"We'll be in touch as soon as we have more information," Detective Graves said.

When they exited, Tia picked up the broken phone the detectives had left. She turned it over in her hands and noticed her nails. Long and acrylic. A sign she took care of her appearance, but the phone gave her nothing more. With a sigh, she set it beside her and turned on the television. The news came on and the story caught her attention.

"Last night the opening of the new local restaurant Fire Dreams was overshadowed by a terrible hit and run accident. The driver of this vehicle survived but remains in intensive care." Tia sucked in her breath as the camera showed the car she was in. The other vehicle must have hit the passenger side which was lucky because her car was a crushed disaster. Had she been in the passenger side, she would not have lived. "The police believe the other driver was in a black Ford truck. If you saw the accident or have any information, you are being asked to call the Fire Beach Police Department."

A red sports car? That must say something about her. She either had money or wanted to appear that she did. What had she been wearing? Tia glanced around the room, but saw no clothes. Had the hospital taken them? She would have to ask when a nurse came in.

Her gaze wandered back to the TV. Would anyone call the number? She hoped they did because right now all she had was a name and an uneasy feeling that someone was out to get her.

BRODY STARED down at the burger and fries he had ordered and sighed. Around him, the restaurant hummed with conversation but he heard none of it. He had hoped leaving the hospital and grabbing some dinner would lift his mood, but it didn't appear to be working so far.

Nick folded himself into the booth across from him and grabbed one of Brody's fries. "Long day?" he asked before shoving the fry in his mouth.

Brody shrugged. "The usual, I guess. I just can't get that woman off my mind."

"The one from the car wreck?" Nick asked when his mouth was clear of food.

"Yeah, she woke up today but has no memory of who she is or what happened to her. I know she's just a patient and she's a little abrasive, but there's something about her. I just feel this need to protect her."

Nick's brow shot up. "Is the self-proclaimed done-with-love Dr. Brody Cavanaugh contemplating giving love another shot?"

Brody rolled his eyes at the name. He had never claimed he was done with love. He had simply not dated since his wife died. Though his friends had tried to get him back out there, no woman had held his interest enough to attempt going out with her. "No, I don't think so. I told you my heart died with Rachel, but something bothers me about this. The accident, her memory loss, the fact that she had no ID with her. Why would someone drive without ID?"

Nick shrugged and grabbed another fry. "Maybe she was just going out for a quick drive and forgot it. I've done that so many times." Brody had no doubt he did. Nick was the epitome of a laid-back surfer dude with his chin length blond hair and blue eyes. His attire consisted mainly of cargo pants, sandals, and chambray shirts, and Brody had never seen him angry. Ever.

"Maybe." But that didn't feel right to Brody. Even when he went out for a quick drive, he always brought his wallet. Sure, there had been the few times he'd forgotten it and maybe that was what had happened to her, but he didn't think so. She'd been dressed for a meeting or a date with her high heeled shoes and designer outfit - not the kind of thing one wore when just out for a drive. Plus, the no ID coupled with the hit and run just seemed too coincidental. "Plus, she also thinks someone was after her."

"Why?"

Brody shook his head. "I don't know. She said she remembered bright lights and being afraid. I was going to call psych to come evaluate her, but then Jordan showed up and said they weren't sure it was an accident. No brake marks on the road. But if it wasn't an accident, then it means someone tried to kill her, and if they come looking to finish the job, we have no idea who we are looking for. Her story was on the news today I heard."

"We have security guards," Nick said with a shrug.

"Yeah, but not enough and they've never been tested." In fact, the security guards were staffed by an outside company and Brody had never seen them do anything except sit at a desk by the exit.

Nick paused his devouring of Brody's fries and cocked his head. "Are you sure you aren't developing feelings for this woman?"

"No," Brody said with a firm shake of his head. "But she does remind me of Rachel. I wasn't able to help her once the cancer took hold, and now I feel the same way about this woman. I mean I can monitor her injuries, but I can't get her memory back. I became a doctor to help people, Nick."

Nick held his hands up in surrender. "All right, I hear you, man." He leaned back and folded his toned tan arms across his broad chest. "So, what do you want to do?"

Finally. Now, he was getting through to his friend. Brody splayed his hands on the table top as he leaned forward. "I want to find out everything we can about this woman. When I made my final check on her, she told me the detectives found out her name was Tia

Sweetchild from the vehicle rental agreement."

"Tia Sweetchild?" Nick rubbed his chin as he said the words thoughtfully. "Why does that name seem familiar to me?" He pulled out his cell phone and began tapping the screen.

"I have no idea." Brody took a sip of his drink. Why hadn't he thought to do that? He could have googled the woman just as easily, but the truth was he rarely used his phone. Nick was about the only person he called anymore. "A previous patient?" His eyes raked over the dinner. He'd box the food up for later. His appetite had suddenly disappeared as his curiosity had taken over.

"Nope." Nick smiled and his eyes held a triumphant gleam. He turned his phone so Brody could see it. "Try romance author."

Brody grabbed the phone and stared closer at the picture. The woman in the hospital was beat up, but the resemblance was there. He looked back at Nick. "You read romance novels?"

Nick scoffed and shook his head. "No way, man, but Erica, that nurse I was trying to date a few months ago, does. She was always reading on her break. I only remember the name because it was different, you know? I thought maybe it was a made-up name. You know like a pen name."

Clearly it wasn't a pen name unless she took it to the point of creating an address in a fake name, but that didn't answer the immediate question. "Why would anyone want to hurt a romance writer?" Brody asked returning his focus to the screen to learn more about Tia.

"My guess is if you find that out, you'll find out who's after her. If someone's after her." Nick took another French fry, and Brody pushed the plate toward him. He could eat at home later. Right now, he needed to find out everything he could about Tia Sweetchild.

CHAPTER 4

"Good morning. Would you care for a pen and some paper?"

Tia opened her eyes to see Dr. Cavanaugh standing over her bed. His hands were behind his back, but his eyes twinkled. Flecks of green and gold danced in them, and she thought she could get used to seeing those eyes gazing at her every day. Well, that was if she wasn't married or already dating someone. "Why would I need pen and paper? I'm not sure I could move enough to use them." Her pain was less intense today, but even with that, a stiffness had settled in much like sore muscles after a hard workout. Hmm, was that just common knowledge or did she have first-hand experience. Did she work out?

"How about a computer then or a dictation machine?" He continued to smile at her as if he had a secret he was bursting to share with her.

While she would love a computer to look up information about herself, she didn't think that's what he was getting at. "Okay, you look like the cat who ate the canary. Why don't you just tell me what this is about?"

"I just thought a romance author might have a reason to write." He brought his hands forward and held out a book to her. The title *True Love* filled the top of the book and underneath was a couple who looked very much in love, but it was the bottom of the book that caught her eye. Tia Sweetchild.

"Is that… is that me? Is that my book?"

He turned the book around to show the back which held a description and an author's photo. The woman on the back was blonde and had a perfect smile, but though she looked happy, her eyes contained a sadness. Had she not been happy? "It sure looks like you," he said, "and I did some research on the author. She lives in California."

"Where the rental agreement said I lived," Tia said softly. She lifted her hand to touch the book hoping it would jog a piece of her memory, but when she touched the cover, she didn't see a happy couple. Instead, she saw angry eyes. "What are you doing here?" With a gasp, she removed her hand.

"What? What is it?" Dr. Cavanaugh asked. Concern replaced the twinkling in his eyes.

"I saw something. A man, and he was furious. He asked me what I was doing there." Tia shook her head slightly wishing she could pull more from her memory.

Dr. Cavanaugh set the book beside her and touched her arm. "Hey, that's a start. We'll start keeping track of what you remember. I'm sure it will all come back eventually. In the meantime, how about I take a look under the bandage and see how your head is healing."

Tia nodded and let him peel the dressing from her head wondering how bad it was. A vague feeling of vanity passed through her. It was obvious from her nails and the car she had been driving that her appearance had been important to her. She supposed as an author, she needed to at least be presentable, but she felt there was more to it than that. "What happened to the clothes I was wearing when I came in?"

"What?"

"The clothes I was wearing. I know I wasn't wearing a hospital gown when I got in the wreck, so where are the clothes I was wearing?"

"Oh, um, I don't know, but I'll check for you. I was there though. At the accident. You were wearing a red designer suit and expensive-looking heels. I had to cut your shoes off. My guess is they cut your suit off when you arrived here."

Designer clothes? Expensive heels? So, she must have money. She wished she could see the clothing to see if it opened any other shut doors in her memory. "Do they throw them away when the cut them off?"

"Sometimes. I'll ask around for you and have Valerie bring them in if she finds them. The cut is looking better by the way. The stitches are holding."

"Stitches? Will I have a scar?" Her voice had taken on a slight shrill irrational edge, but he didn't seem to notice.

"Probably a small one, but don't worry about it. You do feel warm though." He ran the thermometer across her forehead, and his brow furrowed.

"Is it bad?"

"It's one hundred and two. Not great and a little worrisome especially after a concussion and your foot surgery. I'll have Valerie keep a closer eye on you, and I'll check in more often as well." He replaced the bandage and then moved to her foot. "Let's see if you're feeling your toes today."

Tia closed her eyes to focus on his touch. "There," she said when she thought he had touched her toes.

"Good, there's a little sensation today. That's progress. It looks like you'll be staying with us a little longer though."

"It's not like I have anywhere to be," Tia said. "At least I don't think so. Does the biography on the back say anything about a family?"

Dr. Cavanaugh picked up the book and turned it over. "Tia Sweetchild is a clean romance writer who lives in California. When not writing, she enjoys yoga, candlelit dinners, and long walks on the beach."

Yoga. Well that explained the feeling of stiff muscles. Unless she had always been nimble, she was sure she had felt some stiffness when she first started yoga, but candlelit dinners and long walks on the beach? The rest of her biography sounded more like a dating ad than a life.

"It doesn't say anything about a family. I'm sorry." His eyes held her gaze, and something akin to sadness flickered in them.

"Thank you." Tia didn't enjoy hearing those words, but they somehow felt right. She didn't feel like she had any family waiting for her, and the thought saddened her. "What about you? Do you have family?"

His lips pulled into a thin line, and his hand scraped across his chin. "My parents are still alive, though they don't live here. I have an older brother and a younger sister, but as for the family I think you meant...no. I was married, but my wife died a year ago."

"I'm sorry," Tia said. She hadn't meant to open wounds especially with him being so nice to her. A strained silence fell between them. "How old do you think I am?"

"What?" The question had obviously caught Dr. Cavanaugh off guard, and the look on his face displayed his discomfort in trying to answer. "I don't know. Close to thirty maybe?"

Thirty? That meant she was past prime child bearing years and she didn't even have a husband. Did she even want kids? Maybe she had been so focused on her writing that she had decided to forgo a family. That thought saddened her even more.

"Maybe even younger," he said as if sensing her feelings. "I'm a terrible judge of age."

"Oh, it's not that," Tia said. "I just can't believe I'm close to thirty and don't have a family. No one to miss me. It makes me wonder what my priorities were."

"I'm sure your fans miss you," he said. "From the research I did on you, it seems like you have some die-hard fans."

"You researched me?" Tia didn't know why but that thought made her smile. How long had he spent digging into her? And did he do this for every patient with amnesia or was she special? She didn't think she would mind if he found her special. He was definitely easy on the eyes and had a kind air about him. She could see herself dating someone like him – that is if she wasn't seeing someone already.

A red tint colored his cheeks and he cleared his throat as his eyes flicked to the side. "Well, I wanted to have some information to share with you about who you were. Unfortunately, I couldn't find much other than great reviews. You must be a talented writer."

"I hope I remember how to do it again one day." Tia didn't know what she would do if she didn't remember how to write. She had no idea if she possessed any other skills. Had she always been a writer? Was it a full-time job?

"I bet you will." His eyes softened as he gazed at her. "You look like the kind of person who has stories running around in their head."

Tia's heart warmed at his statement, and she felt the corners of her mouth twitch into a flirtatious grin. "I do? What exactly does 'having stories running around in your head' look like?"

She was pleased to see another blush color his face. Had he been flirting with her? "Um, well, there's a depth in your eyes even for someone who doesn't remember who they are. My guess is you've led an interesting life."

"An interesting though private life it seems," she said remembering the lack of information he was able to find out about her. While that might not normally be bad, it certainly didn't help her current situation.

"Maybe you just don't like the fame," he

offered with a crooked smile. Their eyes
locked for a moment before he cleared his
throat and checked his watch. "Anyway, I've
got to go check on a few other patients. I'll
leave the book with you and if you feel up to
it, maybe you can read some. Perhaps that
might help jog your memory."

Tia returned his smile and felt a bud of
warmth erupt in her heart. "Thank you. I
certainly hope so."

BRODY WAS STILL SMILING as he exited Tia's
room. It was nice to be able to help her even
if only a little. He picked up the chart for the
next patient and perused it.

"Don't you think you're spending too
much time with her?"

Brody looked up to see Valerie Givens,
one of the nurses, staring at him. Her arms
were folded across her chest and her brow
arched halfway up her large forehead. Valerie
was a stickler for rules and often interjected
her opinion without asking which made her
amazing at her job but not the easiest person
to get along with. It probably didn't help that
she had indicated an interest in him when

she'd heard his friends were trying to set him up, but he had declined even an initial get together. Dating where he worked held little appeal and she was so stiff that he couldn't imagine spending time with her.

He took a moment to compose his words before he spoke. There was no need to ruffle Valerie's feathers more than he already had. "She has no one. She isn't even sure who she is. I think it's acceptable to try and help her remember a little about herself. Besides as an ICU doctor, that's part of my job description."

Valerie's lips pursed into a tight light. "I know you like to be hands on, especially since your wife died, but are you sure that's all it is? You do remember developing a relationship with a patient is frowned upon."

Brody sighed and rolled his eyes. So was dating coworkers, but that hadn't stopped her from trying. He'd never had this issue when Rachel was alive, but ever since she passed, people had either been trying to set him up or assumed he was flirting with every single woman he came across. It was tiring and flat out wrong. Rachel had been the love of his life, and he wasn't looking to replace her. Not now and, more than likely, not in the future.

Work was his life now, and he was okay with that. "Oh, and Tia has a fever, so keep a close eye on her. I've got other patients to see."

She narrowed her eyes at him but said nothing more, and he turned to enter the next room. Before he reached the door, the familiar voice of Edith Wilkerson reached him.

"Dr. Cavanaugh. Dr. Cavanaugh, can I have a word?"

Edith Wilkerson was seventy years of age, short, and possessed a feisty albeit sometimes abrasive attitude. A little over a year ago, she had begun volunteering to read to patients in the ICU especially those who had no one to visit them. While he appreciated the help, she was often a pain to deal with, but she had been there for Rachel during the days he couldn't.

Pasting on his best smile, he turned to Edith. "Yes, Edith, what can I do for you?"

She waddled over to him and jabbed her finger up at him. "Why is your nurse giving me such a hard time? I've been coming here and reading to patients for over a year." She patted the bag that hung from her shoulder proudly. "Nobody else sits with them that long. You all ought to be thanking me, not shooing me out."

Brody tried not to roll his eyes. "I'm sorry, Edith, I'll have a talk with Valerie." He turned to step back into the room, but she grabbed his arm.

"It wasn't Valerie. She's a pain that one, but she knows better than to talk like that to me. No, it was one I've never seen before. Must be a new one. Italian looking with dark hair."

Brody tried to visualize the women who worked on the floor, but he didn't recognize the woman Edith described. However, it felt like they were always assigning new nurses to the floor or moving them around. "I'm sorry, I'm not familiar with her, but maybe you're right, she could be a new hire. Just tell her you belong here, and I said you're okay to visit the patients. If she has a problem, have her come to me."

"I'll do that. You'd think you all would lay out the carpet for volunteers like me, but no, it's constant scrutiny and questions."

"It is a hospital, Edith," Brody said with a sigh. "We have to make sure our patients are safe."

She threw her hands up and shook her head. "And I look so threatening. Half of the patients here could run faster than I could."

That wasn't true, of course, as most of the patients on this floor were in critical condition, but he understood her sentiment. With her white fluffy hair and short stature, she certainly didn't look menacing. At least, not unless she caught you with her angry gaze. A gaze he'd only seen once, but that reminded him of the look his father had flashed before taking off his belt and whipping Brody with it when he was young. "I'll remind the nurses again, Edith."

"You do that. Now, who should I read to first today?"

As much as Brody didn't want to overwhelm Tia with Edith, she might enjoy the visit since no one had come to see her yet. "Try the woman in six. She lost her memory though, so be nice."

She shot him a pointed stare. "I'm always nice, Dr. Cavanaugh. You of all people ought to know that."

Brody didn't argue with her. Nice was subjective, and it wasn't always the adjective he would apply to Edith, but he did remember how she sat with Rachel while Brody worked. How she kept Rachel company when the pain got bad. How she read to Rachel when her eyesight failed. "Her name is Tia."

"Wonderful. I'll go make her acquaintance."

Brody nodded as he turned to head into the next patient's room, but before he could, a beeping sounded and Valerie popped out of one of the rooms. "Dr. Cavanaugh, we need you in room four."

He spared one final glance at Edith before hurrying to help the crashing patient.

CHAPTER 5

ia smiled as the sound of footsteps entered her room. Was Dr. Cavanaugh back so quickly? Perhaps he had enjoyed their conversation as much as she had and wanted to continue it. Of course, it could be Valerie, the nurse who came in to check her vitals every hour or so, but she hoped it was Dr. Cavanaugh. Valerie was much brusquer and less talkative and either had a permanent chip on her shoulder or just didn't like Tia.

But it was neither. Instead, a short elderly woman with a full head of white hair entered the room. A visitor? She certainly looked too old to be a nurse.

"Can I help you?" Tia asked.

"I'm Edith Wilkerson. I'm a volunteer at the hospital here, and I've come to read to you." The woman did not phrase this as a question but as a matter of fact statement.

"Oh, I didn't realize the hospital did that."

Edith waved her weathered hand as she pulled up a chair. "The hospital doesn't. The Good Lord called me to do this and they tolerate me. Some new nurse even tried to shoo me away today. People have forgotten what God says about caring for the sick and the elderly."

"I'm not sure I know much about that myself." Tia didn't know if she was a church goer or not, but she thought it might be nice to believe in a higher power looking out for her. "What *does* God say about caring for the sick and the elderly?"

"That we should do it. Yet most people nowadays are glued to their electronic devices and rarely bother to think about others." She pulled a book out of her bag and opened it. "Now, I'm in Psalms. Is that okay with you?"

"Um, sure, I suppose." Tia got the feeling that it wouldn't matter to Edith if it wasn't okay with her. The woman looked like she did what she wanted regardless of what others thought, and Tia wondered if she were like that. If not, she thought she might like to be. There was a refreshing honesty to Edith.

Edith pulled out a pair of reader glasses, but before she got very far, another woman entered the room. Tia glanced over but she didn't recognize this brunette woman in cream colored pants and a flowy blouse either. Another visitor? She'd had no one come to see her and now two in one day. What were the odds? Though the woman flashed a smile, her expression seemed more anxious than friendly.

"Oh, I'm sorry, I didn't know you had a visitor already." A slight tremble laced the woman's voice, and she gripped the two bags on her shoulder tighter. Tia wondered if the nervous air the woman exuded was always there or if this situation made her nervous for some reason. Perhaps the nurse had told her Tia might not remember her. That would have to be jarring for anyone.

"I'm not a visitor," Edith said turning shrewd eyes on the woman. "I'm a volunteer."

The woman glanced at Edith before dropping her gaze to the floor. "Oh, well, can I have a moment with Tia?"

"I'm not leaving because I haven't finished my duty, but I'll go sit over there." Edith closed her book and moved to a chair across the room, but her eyes stayed on Tia and the woman.

"Do I know you?" It was a dumb question as the woman had just said her name, but it slipped out before Tia could stop it. She tried to recall any memory of the woman with her mousy brown hair and hazel eyes, but nothing appeared.

"You mean you don't know me?" The woman said the words slowly and her voice held a hint of disbelief, but at that realization, her posture seemed to gain confidence. Her shoulders pulled back and her gaze landed on Tia fully instead of skirting to the side as it had done before.

Something in her gaze bothered Tia but she couldn't put her finger on what it was. "I don't. I hit my head in a car accident, and I don't remember much before waking up here."

"Is that right?" The woman's voice sounded wrong somehow.

Fear bubbled in Tia's stomach, and she narrowed her eyes at the woman. "Are we friends?"

The woman's lips pulled into something close to a smile. "What? Yeah. Friends. I'm

Debra Rearden." She looked at Tia expectantly as if waiting for the name to mean something.

And it did. Slightly. The name triggered something at the back of Tia's mind, something that made her heart beat faster and her pulse speed up, but she couldn't bring the memory forward. "I'm sorry. I still don't know you."

At this, the woman appeared to brighten even more. "Oh, well, I heard about your accident, and I wanted to bring you this." She slid one bag off her shoulder and held it out to Tia.

A memory flashed in Tia's head. She had bought that bag at an upscale boutique in California. She remembered touching the different colorful bags and finally choosing the brown leather because it felt so soft beneath her fingers. "That's my bag."

The woman's smile faltered, and her eyes shifted again. "So, you remember this?"

"I have a vague memory of purchasing it, but nothing more. Why do you have it? The police said it wasn't in my car."

"You left it at my place." The smile returned but it seemed to stop short of Debra's eyes. Their hazel depths contained no fondness, and Tia wondered why. Had they had an argument? "I'm not sure how you forgot it, but I found it on my table. When I saw your accident on the news, I figured you might be missing it." She stepped closer and handed the bag to Tia. Her eyes traveled from Tia's head to her foot. "It appears you'll be here a while."

"Yeah, they haven't given me a release date yet, but I figure it will be another week at least. I guess that's fine since I wouldn't know where to go anyway." Though Debra's behavior struck her as odd, she was also the only outside person who appeared to know her, and Tia hoped she might have some answers. "Do I live here now? They said I'm from California."

Debra's lips pinched together and her eyes flicked away again. Her hand clutched the remaining strap on her shoulder. "I think you were just out here visiting me actually. We hadn't gotten to visit much. Yet," she added hastily as if sensing the oddity of her words. Her eyes flicked quickly to Edith and then back to the floor. "You really don't remember?"

A visit? The feeling she had come to see someone felt right, but she didn't think it was this woman. Why would Tia visit someone and not talk about where she was staying or for how long? Was Debra lying then? Or maybe Tia had been visiting someone in addition to Debra? Still, she had Tia's bag, so at least part of her story was true. "I don't, but thank you for bringing this by. Maybe it will jog some memories."

"Of course, I'm happy to help," Debra said, but her voice held that sappy fake-pleasant tone that people used when they said something they didn't mean. As Tia thought the words, she realized she had used that very tone herself. Often. She couldn't remember exact instances, but she knew she had that delivery down to a tee.

Debra glanced over at Edith and readjusted her bag. "I'll let you get back to whatever I interrupted as I have to run to a meeting, but I'll be back to see you. Soon."

Tia glanced up at Debra with her one good eye. Apprehension filled her as something in Debra's tone bothered her, but she didn't know what it was. "Thank you."

"I don't like her," Edith said when Debra left. "She seems off."

Tia had to agree with her. "She does, but she brought me my purse, so how bad could she be? Maybe this will hold some keys to who I am." She opened the bag and looked inside. Not much was in there: a maroon wallet, a black and gold makeup case, a hairbrush, and a crumpled piece of paper. Not much to go on. She pulled out the wallet first and opened it. The left side held rows of credit cards all in the name Tia Sweetchild. Behind them was a pocket that contained fifty dollars in cash. So, whoever Debra was, she hadn't wanted to steal from Tia. Maybe she really was a friend and hospitals simply made her nervous. On the right were cards for other businesses - a movie theater, a coffee shop, places she must frequent.

Tia pulled out the movie card and held it in her hand. An image of her and a handsome man standing in line to buy tickets flashed into her brain and then disappeared. A date? A relative? She truly had no idea.

She pulled out the coffee card next. A skinny caramel macchiato with no foam? Was that what she drank? Tia replaced the coffee card and pulled out the license. The same blonde woman from the back of the book stared up at her from the license and when she read the address, she could picture a pool, but that was all.

With a sigh, she replaced the wallet and pulled out the makeup bag. It was stuffed with all sorts of makeup - eyeliners in three different colors, four different eyeshadows, two blushes, two mascaras, and four lipstick containers.

"That is a lot of makeup," Edith said as she watched Tia pull everything out. "I gave it up many years ago, but at my age, it isn't really necessary. Not like you young things. You must have liked it a lot."

"I suppose I did." Tia's fingers pulled out a gold plated compact and trembled as she held it. She hadn't asked to see her face, and she wasn't sure she wanted to, but the need to spurred her fingers. As the mirror lifted, Tia sucked in her breath. The face staring back at her didn't look much like the woman in the picture. Angry bruises and red raw scrapes covered most of her face. A large white bandage blazed out from the top of her left forehead, and her left eye was a black and purple mottled mess. She shut the mirror not wanting to see any more, but she couldn't stop the tear that trickled out of her right eye. "I'm so hideous."

Edith placed a wrinkled hand on her arm. "You are not hideous. You are a beautiful creature in God's eyes and whatever scars you may have from this accident, they don't have to define you."

Tia nodded, but Edith's words didn't replace the sickening feeling in her stomach. Everything she had learned about herself from her nails to her makeup was that image was important to her. What would she do if she was scarred for life? After replacing the makeup bag, she bypassed the hairbrush and pulled out the crumpled paper. Rico Rearden, six pm, 144 Palisade Drive. Rico Rearden? An image of a house exploded in her head, and she dropped the paper. She had been meeting Rico Rearden, not Debra, but the question was for what? And who was Rico Rearden?

"Are you okay?" Edith asked squeezing her arm.

"No, I don't think that I am," Tia said.

BRODY OPENED his fridge and stared at the scant offerings. He really needed to get better about going to a store, or he should break down and hire an assistant like Nick had. Nick had a woman who bought for him, laid out ingredients for dinner, and straightened up. With as much as he worked, Brody should do the same, but having another woman in his house, even just to shop and do meal prep, felt like an affront to Rachel.

He still remembered coming home to her each night. The smell of whatever she was cooking would greet him as he walked in the door tantalizing his taste buds and sending his stomach growling. Rachel had been a fantastic cook.

He would drop his work gear by the front door, then he would wander into the kitchen and greet her by wrapping his arms around her waist and nuzzling her neck. She would pretend to bat him away with whatever cooking utensils she had in her hands, but he knew she loved the attention. After dinner, they would wash the dishes together trading secret smiles and glances when their fingers touched. Then they would retire to the bedroom where they would read or watch television before falling asleep in each other's arms.

Brody hadn't been able to sleep in the bed for a month after Rachel passed. It held too many memories. Many nights, he still crashed on the couch though recently that was due more to exhaustion from work than anything else.

With a sigh, he shut the fridge door. He would order pizza again and see if Nick wanted to swing by. Lately, it was how they spent most nights after work. Either his place or Nick's or out. Except on the nights when Nick had a date.

Brody wondered if he would ever date again. He'd thought about it once or twice after Rachel's death, but after having someone so amazing, he could tell just by meeting a woman that they would never measure up. But he was still young. And he knew Rachel would want him to find someone to spend his life with. His thoughts drifted to Tia.

What must it be like to wake up and have no memory of who you were? In his own case, he couldn't decide if that would be a good thing or a bad thing. On one hand, he would have no painful memory of Rachel's death, but on the other hand, he would have no loving memory of Rachel in his life either. It was better to have loved and lost than never to have loved at all. Wasn't that what the old saying was?

Brody shook his head to clear the fog. He was too philosophical tonight. He should skip the pizza and the conversation and just grab something quick. There was a restaurant just down the street that stayed open late. He would grab dinner and one drink and then return to bed. Before he could change his mind, he exited the house, locked the front door behind him, and headed down the street.

The restaurant was busy when he opened the door, but he managed to find an empty barstool.

"What'll you have?" the bartender asked as he sat down.

Brody surveyed the drink selection. He wasn't a big drinker, but he and Rachel had partaken on occasion. "A Sam Adams?"

With a nod, the bartender turned and grabbed a bottle, popped the lid, and handed it to Brody. "You want to open a tab?"

Brody pondered the question. He'd told himself he would just have one, but now that he was here, he wasn't sure. He was about to agree when a voice beside him said, "No need. It's on me." He looked up to see Detective Graves standing next to him. "Grab that and follow me."

Curious, he followed Jordan to an empty booth. "Were you following me, detective?"

"No, but I'm glad I ran into you. Did our patient remember anything more today?"

Brody shook his head. He had checked on Tia before his shift ended, but she hadn't said much. "No, but I didn't really ask today. I did find out she is an author though and I brought in one of her books hoping it would help."

Jordan's eyes narrowed. "How did you find out she was an author?"

"I had dinner with Nick last night and he recognized her name, so we googled her. Anyway, when I showed her the book, she said she remembered something when she touched it." He paused, trying to remember her words. "A man saying 'What are you doing here?' But that was all she could remember. She didn't even remember being an author. Should I be asking specific questions? Did you find something out?"

Jordan blew out an agitated breath. "Not much more than that, but it just isn't sitting well with me. Why would anyone want to harm an author? She's not a big name like Stephen King or J.K Rowling so I don't think it was about money, and she writes clean romance so I doubt she offended someone enough to want to kill her. All I have are questions - the biggest one being what was she doing here in the first place?"

"I don't know." Brody shook his head and took a sip of his beer. He had his own questions, but they were more about the woman herself than why she had come to Fire Beach in the first place. "She said a woman visited her today and claimed she was in town for that reason."

Jordan's head snapped forward. "What? She had a visitor?"

"Yes, she didn't remember the woman, but she hasn't remembered much. Why? Is that a bad thing?"

Agitation filled Jordan's face. "It could be. We asked her to call us if anything else happened. We need to know everything if we are going to figure this out. I can't believe she didn't tell us she had a visitor. Did you get the woman's name?"

Brody shook his head. "No, sorry, I was a little busy, but I can ask tomorrow."

"I'll go over myself tomorrow to ask, but please, Brody, we can't help if we don't know everything. Even if it seems trivial."

Brody gave a curt nod. He was glad Jordan was helping, but he didn't like someone telling him to do his job. "I understand. It seems she gets a few pieces of her memory back every day. Maybe we'll know more in a day or two."

"Let's hope that's soon enough, but please keep an eye on her and call me if you learn anything. I just have a bad feeling about all of this."

ia couldn't wait to see Dr. Cavanaugh today. She was bursting at the seams to tell him she had remembered a little more about her past. Specifically, that she was from Texas and her mother had a strong southern drawl. The memory had come to her as she was watching Sweet Home Alabama on the TV the night before, and while an Alabama accent wasn't the same as a Texas drawl, there were similarities.

"Well, don't you look chipper today," Dr. Cavanaugh said as he entered her room.

Her lips split in a wide smile. "I am. I remembered a little more of my past. I'm originally from Texas." She said the words proudly as if they were a star achievement which in her case, they sort of were.

"Is that right?" His eyes did that twinkly thing that set her heart fluttering as he returned her grin. "So, a girl from Texas, living in California, but out in Illinois. Maybe you like to travel?" He raised a brow at her as he checked her chart.

"Maybe or maybe not." She watched him move to the IV to check the levels.

"Detective Graves wasn't too happy that you didn't call him about your visitor."

Tia dropped her gaze. "I know. He's already been here this morning. Reamed me pretty good, but I honestly didn't think about it. She said she was a friend and I was in town visiting her. It's not like I would know differently. Detective Graves also took my purse and the note."

Brody's head snapped toward her. "Note? What note?"

Oh right, she hadn't told him about the note either. "I went through my purse when she brought it back and I found a note in my purse with a man's name on it. I feel like I was visiting him, but I don't know why."

"Perhaps he's someone you're seeing?" Was she imagining his smile looking a little more forced as he asked those words? Was he upset at the thought of her seeing someone? "Regardless, I bet you'll remember soon, and I'm sure Detective Graves will look into him. You did tell him about your feeling, right?"

"Yes, I told him." Tia felt like a child being scolded. First Detective Graves had jumped on her case and now Dr. Cavanaugh.

"Good. I'm going to change the bandage on your head now."

As he removed the bandage from her head, Tia tried not to focus on the strong angle of his chin or how his touch sent her heart skidding in her chest. She wondered what his beard would feel like under her fingertips? Would it be rough and bristly or softer? And if she touched it, would he lean into her hand or bat it away? He'd told her of his wife's death, but she hadn't asked if he were single still.

"You know what? The stitches are healing nicely. I think it's time they got some air."

His voice brought her back to reality, and she struggled to keep her voice from betraying her thoughts. "That's good, right?"

"It's excellent." His eyes caught hers and Tia's breath stilled. There was something in his gaze. Something more than a doctor caring for a patient. She was sure of it. Should she say something? Ask him if he was single? "Look at that, your left eye is open a little too."

Her breath tumbled out in a sigh, and a tinge of sadness filled her. Of course, he was looking at her eye. He was her doctor, nothing more. She would do good to remember that.

"The cuts on your arms appear to be healing nicely too."

"How much longer until I'm released, do you think?" She didn't really want the answer, but felt like she should ask it. With still so much of her life unknown, she felt more comfortable just staying at the hospital and seeing Dr. Cavanaugh every day. When she left, would she have a reason to see him again?

"I'm not sure," he said as he ran the thermometer across her forehead. "While you are healing nicely on the outside, I am still concerned about your memory and though the fever has gone down, it is still slightly above normal. Plus, Dr. North will probably want to look at your foot again before she releases you. Speaking of which, we should check your foot." He finished examining her legs and touched her toes. "Can you feel that?"

Tia smiled as she felt his fingers. This time she didn't have to guess. "I can. Just barely, but I can."

"Excellent. That is what I like to hear." He made a few notes in the chart and then turned his full attention back to her. "Did you read your book yesterday?"

Tia glanced at the book on the table next to her bed. "A little, but reading with only one eye was giving me a headache. I probably should have asked Edith to read that to me instead of the Bible. Maybe I'll try again today though and see if it helps me remember any more."

Dr. Cavanaugh smiled and touched her arm. "I think that is a great idea. I'll be back to check on you later." His fingertips pressed just slightly on her arm. Only the slightest hint of pressure, but Tia felt there was more there than a simple touch.

As he walked out of her room, she rolled her eyes. She was seeing romance where there was none. Perhaps she could write again. Maybe this was why she had become a romance author in the first place.

She grabbed the book off the table and

opened it to try reading some more, but she had only gotten through a few pages when footsteps in her doorway grabbed her attention. Tia looked up to see Debra in her room again, but this time the smile was gone and a cold gleam shone from her eyes.

"What's wrong, Debra?" Tia inched her finger up toward the call button. Perhaps it was nothing, but Debra's expression was setting off alarm bells in her body.

"Wrong? Nothing's wrong. I've just come here to finish business." Her voice was as cold and soulless as her eyes.

Fear raced through Tia's veins and she placed her finger on the button. She would press it, but she needed answers first. "Business? What are you talking about? I thought you said we were friends."

Debra's expression turned into a snarl. "Friends?" she spat before issuing a derisive laugh. "Friends don't sleep with their friend's husband."

"What?" Tia's body froze. She hated that she had little memory, but she couldn't imagine herself doing that. "I would never..."

Debra cut her off with biting words that carried their own weapons. "How do you know what you would never do? You told me yesterday you had no memory."

"I may not remember much, but I don't think I would do that." The thought of that sent such revulsion through her that Tia couldn't believe it was true.

"You don't think...." Condescension dripped from Debra's voice like venom. "Do you want to know where I found the purse that I returned to you yesterday?"

Tia fought to remain calm. "You told me I left it on a table in your house."

Debra's predatory smile widened creating an effect much like The Joker's signature smile on her face. "Yes. On the table in *my* bedroom. So, if you weren't sleeping with my husband, how do you propose it got there?"

"I have no idea, obviously."

"Well, then I guess my version is the only one that matters, but I'm done being the cheated-on wife." From within the bag, she withdrew a gun and with shaky hands, she pointed it at Tia.

Tia pressed the call button hoping someone would see or hear it before Debra shot her. She had no idea if the woman was a good shot or if the obvious nervousness would allow her to miss, but Tia couldn't move, so rescue was her only option.

"Why did you say we were friends?" Tia asked hoping to buy a little time.

"I needed an excuse to see what room you were in and check out the security at the hospital. I had planned to kill you yesterday, but then you had that busybody old woman in here, so I had to adjust my plan. We'd never officially met, so I didn't think you would recognize me unless you paid attention to the pictures of me all over the house, but you were probably too busy with my husband to do that, weren't you?"

Another image flashed into Tia's mind, and she saw herself picking up a picture of Debra and Rico. "You're married? Why did you invite me up here if you were married?"

"You never said it bothered you," he said stepping closer to her.

"Put the gun down, ma'am." Dr. Cavanaugh's voice brought both relief and frustration as the flashback she had been seeing vanished from her mind.

Debra turned to look at him briefly before returning her attention to Tia. "No. She slept with my husband, and now she's going to pay."

"I know how distressing that can be, but is it worth spending the rest of your life in prison?" Dr. Cavanaugh's voice was calm, and he inched toward Debra slowly.

"She deserves to die."

"If she did what you claim, then she deserves punishment, yes, but retribution is not ours to dole out." Tia looked at him. She hoped he didn't really believe Debra's words; she couldn't stand the thought of him thinking so poorly of her.

"She did," Debra screeched shrilly and the hand holding the gun began to shake. "I found her purse in my bedroom. I've known he was having an affair for a while. Always off on his 'business meetings' but I never knew who it was until I found her purse."

"Debra, is your husband's name Rico?" Tia asked. She knew without asking the question that it was, but she hoped to draw Debra's attention long enough for Brody to overpower her.

"You know it is." She glanced quickly at Tia before returning her gaze to Dr. Cavanaugh. "You see? She admits it."

"I don't remember him," Tia said though that was a tiny lie. She had remembered talking to him just now, but there was no need to share that, "and I definitely don't recall sleeping with him, but I found a crumpled piece of paper in my purse with his name and a time on it."

Hesitation flickered in Debra's eyes, but she didn't lower the gun. "That proves it then. You were meeting with him."

"That only proves a meeting," Dr. Cavanaugh said. "Perhaps they were meeting about something else."

"In my bedroom?" A hysterical edge colored her voice, and she took a deep breath. "No, she was sleeping with him, and if I don't punish her, who will?" Her hand wavered as she turned to look at Tia again. It wasn't long, but it was long enough for Dr. Cavanaugh to knock the gun out of her hands and tackle her to the ground.

"What are you doing?" Debra screamed as she writhed on the ground. "She's the criminal, not me."

A moment later, security rushed in and handcuffed Debra before leading her out of the room. Her screams carried down the hall and echoed in Tia's ears long after she was gone.

"Are you okay?" Dr. Cavanaugh asked coming to Tia's side.

Tia ignored his question - he could see that she hadn't been physically injured - and posed her own in return. "What's going to happen to her?"

"I don't know. They'll take her to the police and I'm sure Detective Graves will see if she owns a black Ford truck or knows someone who does. It certainly sounds as if she had a vendetta for you."

Her eyes found his, and she stared into the depths that had once held kindness and now held questions. "Do you think I really did that? What she said?" She needed him not to believe it. Tia still didn't feel that behavior was like her, but the purse was hers and the crumpled paper proved she'd scheduled a meeting with the woman's husband. Plus, there had been that tidbit she'd remembered. She thought she'd sounded angry and confused at finding out he was married, but she couldn't explain why her purse would have been in the woman's bedroom if something illicit wasn't going on.

"I... don't know. It's not my place to judge anyway." The question clearly made Dr. Cavanaugh uncomfortable, and he steered his gaze away from her face. "Did she say anything else to you?"

Tia closed her eyes and tried to remember the words. "Just that she came yesterday to see what the security in the hospital was like and to see if I would recognize her name. She planned to kill me yesterday, but Edith was in here." Tia couldn't keep the intense sadness and disgust out of her voice. "What kind of a person was I?"

Dr. Cavanaugh cleared his throat and ran the back of his fingers down his cheek. "Maybe it's not what it seems. You said you had a paper with meeting details?"

"Yeah, his name, address, and a time."

"Well, I'm no expert, but I don't know many people who schedule trysts like that, so maybe he was an associate or something."

He was guessing, making up options to make her feel better, but Tia appreciated the effort. "Even if he was an associate, I don't know why I'd be in his bedroom which is where she claimed she found my purse."

Dr. Cavanaugh opened his mouth as if to speak, but no words came out.

"It's okay," Tia continued. "You should get back to your other patients. I'm fine now."

"Of course. Call if you need anything." Though they were the same words he often said before leaving, they sounded different this time and Tia couldn't help feeling saddened by the fact she had disappointed him.

BRODY STOOD outside the police station gathering his courage to go in. He didn't even know why he was here especially if Debra's words were true, but the need to help Tia still burned strong within him. Rachel had often accused him of having a 'knight in shining armor complex' and perhaps she had been right because here he was trying to defend a woman who might have been in an affair. He supposed she could have had a different personality before the accident – it certainly happened with traumatic brain injuries - but he just didn't believe the woman in his hospital could have done what Debra claimed.

Before he could grasp the handle, the door swung open and Jordan stared at him from the other side. "Brody? What are you doing here?"

"I was hoping I could talk to you about Tia and the woman from the hospital earlier."

Jordan looked over his shoulder and then back at Brody. "Not here. I'm headed over to

Fire Dreams. Meet me there and I'll tell you what I know, but it isn't much."

Brody nodded and returned to his car. Not much was better than what he knew now which consisted of more questions than answers.

Ten minutes later he sat in a booth with Jordan, a glass of water in front of each of them and a basket of chips in the middle. The place was hopping having recovered nicely from the spoiled opening a few days before and Jordan kept glancing around as if realizing he should be helping rather than sitting and talking.

"So, the lady from the hospital is indeed Debra Rearden. If you or Tia had told us about her yesterday, we could have looked into her sooner. She's clean, but her husband, Rico, has a few questionable connections."

"What kind of questionable connections?" Brody asked.

"On paper, he's the head of a publishing company which might explain the connection to Tia, but we've found some unusual activity with some known drug dealers. Nothing that points to him being directly involved, and Narcotics has never been able to pin anything on him, but we're widening our search to be sure."

Brody nodded and snagged a chip. "Drugs? Really?" This image just didn't jive with the woman he'd gotten to know the last few days. "Tia said she had a meeting with Rico, but she doesn't seem like the type to be into drug deals."

Jordan took a sip of his water. "Maybe she isn't, but I did a little more research on her today. It appears she stayed under the radar. At least recently. Evidently a few months ago, she kind of lost it after trying to damage the reputation of a fellow romance author, Ava McDermott. She sent photos to tabloids and appeared on a few talk shows claiming the relationship Ava was in was a fake one. I don't know why anyone would fake a relationship, but maybe if you are a public figure, it's more important."

"What?" Brody knew he didn't know Tia well, and she could have been awful before the accident, but he couldn't fathom the sweet Texas girl doing such a thing. Oh dear, did he just call her sweet? Maybe he *was* becoming attached to her.

Jordan shrugged. "Well, maybe the head injury changed her or maybe she changed after the incident. She failed to do much except soil her own reputation. Regardless, it's clear Tia did know Rico. There's no other reason Debra would have come after her. Perhaps she was talking to him about new publishing opportunities. We just don't know any more than that."

"Is there a chance she was having an affair with him as his wife claimed?" Brody asked before taking a drink of his water. He didn't want this to be true. He knew Tia was just a patient. And she lived in California. *And* he shouldn't care about her personal life, but he did.

"That I can't speak to. Yet. But we'll be looking into Rico more." Jordan shook some salt on a chip before stuffing it into his mouth.

"And what about the black truck. Did it belong to Debra?"

Jordan shook his head as he finished chewing. "No, neither she nor her husband appear to own one."

"So, someone might still be after Tia."

"It's possible or it could just be that the accident was just that. An accident."

"But you don't believe that, do you?" Brody asked.

"No, I don't. It's just a gut feeling, but I

don't. I've talked with the hospital about posting a security guard outside her door as well." Jordan looked around again and waved at someone across the room. "I have to help out here, but I promise to keep you in the loop of what we find."

"Thank you." Brody stayed and ate a late dinner alone, but his thoughts weren't on the food. They were on the blonde woman whose present didn't seem to match her past.

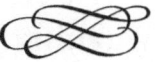

"ou know he's not interested in you romantically, right?"

Tia glanced over at Valerie who held a vase of flowers in her hand. "I'm sorry, what?"

She set the vase down, plucked the card, and handed it to Tia before leaning back and folding her arms across her chest. "Dr. Cavanaugh. He's not interested in you. He doesn't date. Not since his wife died, and he certainly doesn't get involved with patients."

"I never said he was," Tia said. She picked up the card wondering who the flowers were from and why Valerie was bringing this up. The woman had never been overly friendly, but she'd always been professional. This wasn't.

"Maybe not, but you have the look in your eye. That moony starry-eyed look when you talk about him or when you look to the doorway. I'm just warning you those feelings will only end in heartbreak."

Ah, now it made sense. Somehow Dr. Cavanaugh had broken her heart. Had they dated? Or had Valerie simply wished they had? Was it before his wife? Or had he gone on a few dates after her death? "Well, thank you for the information, but Dr. Cavanaugh is my doctor. Nothing more." Though Tia could not deny she imagined something more. She had imagined what it would feel like to touch his face, to run her fingers through his hair, to kiss his lips.

"Mmmhmm." Valerie said nothing more as she ran the thermometer over Tia's forehead and wrote the information down, but her eyes spoke volumes. "I'll send Sophie in later to do another sponge bath."

Relief that Valerie would not be doing her sponge bath filled Tia along with the sudden urge to request another nurse. She was the patient here, and she didn't need a nurse casting a critical eye on her. Tia had enough on her plate trying to remember who she was and why someone might want to hurt her. She opened the card and stared at the writing inside. Or perhaps the lack of writing inside because all that was on the card was the picture of a face with its eyes and mouth stitched shut.

"Good morning. How about we try to get you moving some today?" Dr. Cavanaugh asked as he entered Tia's room. At the sight of her face, his smile faltered and concern filled his voice. "What's the matter?"

Tia held the card out to him. "This came on the flowers Valerie brought in this morning."

Dr. Cavanaugh took the card and opened it. His face paled and his eyes widened as he took in the image. "Where are the flowers?"

Tia pointed over to the table where Valerie had set them. He picked them up, sniffed them, and poked through them as if looking for any other clues. "I'm going to call Detective Graves. He needs to know about this." He pulled a phone from his pocket. "I'll have Valerie come in and take you for a walk."

"No, please not Valerie. Anyone but Valerie." Not only was panic coursing through her veins at the note, but she didn't think she could handle any more time with Valerie.

He paused and caught her eye. "What's wrong with Valerie?"

"She abrasive and she just…" Tia paused. She wasn't sure she wanted to tell Brody what Valerie had said.

"She just what?"

"She just rubbed me the wrong way. In fact, I was going to ask if I could get a new nurse." She didn't know why she didn't tell him the whole truth. Except that she was afraid her attraction would be evident in her words. And she wasn't sure she could take it if he didn't feel the same."

"I'll see what I can do. I know Valerie can be brusque at times, but she is an efficient nurse."

Tia watched his face as he spoke. Did he care about Valerie? Or was he just being professional? Before she could ponder the issue much longer, he stepped toward her.

"I'll tell you what. Let me call Jordan, and then I'll take you for a quick walk today, and we'll figure tomorrow out when it comes."

"Can you do that?" He normally only entered her room twice during the day – once in the morning and once in the evening.

"I'm your doctor. I can take you for a walk if I desire." His jaw tightened and she wondered if there was more to it. Was he worried about her safety as well? "Just give me a second."

He stepped back and then punched numbers into his cell phone, turning slightly away from her as he put it to his ear. "Jordan? It's Brody. Tia received some flowers this morning, and I think you need to come and see the card." He glanced back at her. "Yes, I'm going to take her for a short walk, and then we'll be back.... Got it." He pocketed the phone and then smiled at her. "Ready to go then?"

Though Tia was excited to get out of the bed and move a little, she also worried about her safety and her appearance. She hadn't showered in days though Sophie had given her a sponge bath yesterday. Still, her hair was a greasy mess, and she probably smelled. Sponge baths were like trying to clean an entire house with one wet wipe. "I must look a fright."

"You look.... fine." He paused, and she glanced at him. Did he feel an attraction to her? Though Valerie claimed he wasn't interested, there had been many moments like these. Moments where she caught his eyes and unsaid words passed between them. "Especially for someone who had to be rescued with the Jaws of Life," he continued.

Though not entirely a compliment, Tia decided to take it as one. "What about my leg though? Can I walk on it?"

"Uh no." He chuckled and shook his head. "Today we are just going to try getting you into a wheelchair and out of this room. Then we'll talk about crutches."

"But I don't see a wheelchair," Tia said, and she wondered how she was supposed to get into it without exposing herself with her open-backed gown.

Dr. Cavanaugh flashed her a charming smile. "Ah, just you wait. I have one on order." He walked over to the cabinet in the room and pulled out a robe. "And I think this one is just your size."

She realized he was giving it to her as a way to cover up her bare back, and relief flooded her.

"Let me help you sit up, and then we'll get this robe on you. It will pull on your IV a little, so please tell me if it bothers you. Your transportation should arrive about the time we're finished."

Tia couldn't help the smile that crossed her lips, but it was short lived as Dr. Cavanaugh pulled her to a sitting position. Her hand squeezed his arm, her fingers digging into his flesh, as the room began to spin from lying down for too long and the injury to her head.

"It's okay. We'll go slow," he said. His mouth was close to her ear, and his breath sent a shudder down her back that she hoped he interpreted as her being cold.

She nodded and when the room stayed still, she continued the process of sitting up. Tia was sure she had done this a thousand times in her life, but today it took all of her energy and concentration. When she was fully upright, he helped guide her arms into the robe and she saw for the first time the damage she had received to them. Cuts and bruises discolored her right arm, and again she briefly wondered if she would have scars.

The aide with the wheelchair showed up as she tied the robe in front of her, and Dr. Cavanaugh grinned. "See, what did I tell you? I'll take it from here, Eric. Can you let Valerie know I'm taking my break?"

"Sure, Dr. Cavanaugh."

His break? He was using his break time to

take her out? What would Valerie think of that? Had he ever spent his break time with her? Tia blinked the thoughts away. She needed to focus less on Dr. Cavanaugh and more on her recovery.

He wheeled the chair as close to the bed as possible and then helped her stand. Again, she had to take a moment and clutch onto his shoulder before she could lower herself into the chair. Then he grabbed her IV pole and brought it around to her. "Can you hang onto this?"

She grabbed the pole and pulled it beside her as he wheeled her out of the room. Her eyes glanced around for Valerie and she was glad not to see her in the immediate vicinity, but she was surprised to see the security guard outside her room. He stood as they passed.

"Excuse me, sir, but where are you going?"

"I'm taking Ms. Sweetchild out for some air. Don't worry, I've already cleared it with Detective Graves. You can call him and check for yourself."

The security guard looked as if he were about to argue, but after a moment of exchanging stares with Dr. Cavanaugh, he nodded and then took out his phone.

BRODY DIDN'T KNOW what he was doing taking her out in the middle of the day. It wasn't technically against policy, but it certainly wasn't necessary. Yes, he wanted to share what he had learned last night from Jordan and see if it helped jog her memory at all, but he could have done that in her room. Maybe it was his complex kicking in again, maybe it was the note she had received, maybe it was her reaction to Valerie. Maybe it was just the fact that for the first time since Rachel's death, he felt something for a woman. He wasn't sure it was attraction. Perhaps it was just concern, but it *was* something.

As he wheeled her down the hall, he could feel the eyes of the nurses on him. There would be retribution for this in the form of their gossip and curious gazes for a few days, but he could handle that.

"Where are we going," she asked as he took a detour from the hallway.

"To get some fresh air. I think you could use some." He pushed open the door to a little covered patio on the south side of the hospital and wheeled her toward the lone bench that sat in the concrete area just outside the door. The air was warm but a light breeze floated through stirring the crunchy leaves on the concrete and creating a rustling sound. He wondered if she would be warm enough. He should have asked if she wanted a blanket. They kept some in a warmer by the door. He would remember that next time. Next time? Why was he already thinking about next time with Tia? What was it about her that kept her on his mind? Was it just her memory loss? Was it his need to protect her? Or was there more?

After making sure the brakes were locked on her wheelchair, he sat down on the bench and faced her. "I spoke with Detective Graves last night, and I thought you might want to know what he told me."

Her lips parted in a slight smile before sadness crossed her face. "Why are you doing this for me? If what that woman said is true, I'm not a very nice person."

Brody understood why she would feel that way but it bothered him that she did. Everyone made mistakes, and he couldn't imagine the woman before him doing anything like that now. He also knew the information he was about to share wouldn't make her feel any better, but if he were in her position, he would want to know all of it. The good and the bad. Knowing it all was the only way to make a change going forward. "Does the name Ava McDermott ring a bell for you?"

"Ava McDermott?" Tia turned the name over in her mouth like a fine wine and her eyes stared into space as if searching for images to apply to the name. Then suddenly her eyes lit up. "I do remember an Ava McDermott. She's a…" she paused for a moment as if having to coax the memory forward. "She's a romance writer like me, isn't she?"

Brody nodded. "She is."

"I remember…" Tia's face fell, and her gaze dropped to her hands. "Oh no, I remember being condescending to her at a ceremony for coming without a date. In fact, I think I was rather haughty quite often, but I feel like Ava and I might have been friends at one point."

Brody doubted they were friends now, but he didn't tell her that. Her remembering Ava was a step in the right direction, and he didn't want to push her too hard. "Do you remember anything else about her? Anything more recently?"

Tia pursed her lips together. "I don't, but I'm guessing I'm not going to like the sound of what I did."

"Probably not, but it might explain what you're doing here." Brody took a deep breath as he thought about how best to tell her. "Evidently, you tried to ruin her reputation by outing her to tabloids for what you thought was a fake relationship."

Tia closed her eyes and sighed. "Maybe I don't want to remember my past. I don't sound very nice."

Brody had had the same thoughts when Jordan told him the story. Even now, he was having a hard time imagining the woman in front of him running to the tabloids. "Maybe the accident is God's way of giving you another chance. I have to say that even though I've only known you a few days, I can't see you doing those things now."

"Is that because of the brain injury?" Tia asked.

"It could be. Brain injuries can often change the personality of the patient." He watched her face fall. "But it could also be that you are changing."

"Do you really believe in God?" The simple question held none of the condescension he usually felt when people posed that question.

Brody hadn't been to church in a while, not since Rachel's death, but they had gone regularly when she was alive, and he did still believe. "I do though I can't say I've been a great Christian since my wife died. We used to attend every Sunday, but that stopped when she got sick. And though I know the importance of community in the church, I haven't been back much." He ran a hand across his chin. "Still, as a doctor, I have seen too many things I can't explain, so to answer your question, yes I do believe in God."

"I feel like I did at one time too. Do you think He forgives even people like me?"

"Hey." Brody grabbed her hands. "First of all, you don't know everything. And everyone has parts of their past they wish they could redo or forget. That's normal. What we do about it is ask for forgiveness and strive to be better. You have this amazing opportunity before you to completely change your direction in life."

He paused as he realized he was still holding her hands and the warmth from them was taming the gnawing ache in his soul. Her eyes locked on his, and so much emotion flashed in them. Fear, longing, hope, desire. Though a solid blue color, the emotions they conveyed were like a quilt of many different fabrics sewn together. He should let go of her hands; he had no business falling for her, but he found he didn't want to. Still, if someone came outside and saw them…. With great effort, he cleared his throat and dropped her hands, moving his to his pants leg. "How about Rico Rearden? Did you remember any more about him?"

She tilted her head at him, and her gaze tore through him. Could she see the effect she was having on him? Finally, she shook her head. "Nothing more than I was meeting with him about something, but I can't remember what."

Brody supplied her with the little information he knew in hopes it would help her. "He owns a publishing company, so perhaps you were meeting with him about that?"

A pained expression covered Tia's face. "I don't know. I remember calling him and asking for an appointment, but I don't remember what happened after."

Brody could tell she was getting frustrated, and his break was over anyway. It was time to return her to her room and finish his rounds. "Well, Detective Graves is still looking into both Rico and Debra. Neither appear to have a black truck, so even though you are fearful of what you will remember, getting your memory back is vitally important. Someone might still be after you."

CHAPTER 8

*D*etective Graves was in the room when they returned. "Where do these flowers come from?" he asked.

"From the gift shop downstairs usually or from outside sources," Dr. Cavanaugh said as he wheeled Tia back to the bed.

"And how do they get delivered?"

Dr. Cavanaugh held out his hand and helped Tia stand and get situated back in the bed. "An orderly generally brings them to the floor and then either delivers them or gives them to the nurses to deliver."

"Valerie brought mine in," Tia supplied.

Detective Graves glanced over at her before turning his attention back to Dr.

Cavanaugh. "I'm going to need to speak with her as well."

"Fine, I'll introduce you." Dr. Cavanaugh turned back to Tia. "I'll check on you before I leave for the night."

Tia nodded, but she didn't really feel like being alone. Even the security guard outside her door didn't make her feel much safer. The flowers had still gotten to her, and what if they put anthrax or some kind of air borne poison on them next time. She supposed that was unlikely, but it could happen, right?

Plus, she had the information Dr. Cavanaugh had shared with her rattling around in her head. She'd had enough glimpses of her past to know that she had turned from a sweet Texas girl into a haughty nightmare of a woman, but she couldn't believe she had tried to damage someone's reputation. And while she agreed with Brody that it was important to remember her past for her current safety, she didn't want to think about what an awful person she might have been. Was he right? Was this why this accident had happened to her? Was she being given a second chance? If she was, maybe it would be better if she didn't remember her past.

"Hello, dear, would you like me to read to you some more today?"

Tia looked up to see Edith in the doorway. She held the Bible in her hands and a kind smile graced her face. "Do you come read to patients every day?"

Edith waddled into the room. "Not every day. I have Bridge on Mondays and square dancing on Thursdays, but I try to come on Tuesdays and Wednesdays and some Fridays if my health allows and I don't miss the bus."

Square dancing? This woman certainly seemed spry for someone so old.

"But you didn't answer my question. Would you like me to read to you?"

Tia glanced at the book Brody had brought her yesterday. "Yes, but can you read me that?" She pointed to the book on the table beside her.

Edith picked up the book and raised an eyebrow. "True Love? Is this some sappy romance?"

"Maybe." Tia shrugged. "I don't know. It appears I wrote it, but I don't remember it."

"Well, I don't normally read romances, but since you wrote it, I'll give it a shot. If there are any heaving chests or panting of breaths in here, I stop though. Is that understood?" Edith flashed her a look that Tia imagined was the one she used when she reprimanded her children growing up. If she had any.

Tia nodded and smiled. "I don't think I wrote those kind of romances, but agreed." Having Edith read a scene like that out loud sounded just as mortifying to Tia as it must to Edith.

"Gayle climbed under her desk as the sound of her father's angry footsteps carried down the hall…"

Suddenly, another piece of her past opened up. Tia saw herself curled under a desk where the chair normally sat. A blanket, held in place by the middle drawer, blocked the outside world and allowed her to believe she couldn't be seen. A book lay open on her knees and she held a flashlight in one hand. She was reading. Reading under her desk to hide from her father.

Her father who had never wanted her. Who had told her she should have been a boy. Who had left when she was ten years old because he didn't feel like being a dad any longer. Then her mother appeared. A woman with shoulders rolled forward from heavy work but kind eyes. A woman who had worked two jobs to provide for her and never complained. Tia saw the times her mother cried in her room when she thought Tia wasn't watching. Cried because she didn't have enough money to purchase groceries to feed Tia.

Tia sucked in a breath. That's why she had started writing. She had hoped it would earn enough income that she could take care of her mother. Her teachers had always told her in school that she was creative - probably because she'd had to invent worlds to escape from her father's angry words. So, when had she changed? When had she gone from wanting to write to help her mother to obsessing about her career so much that she was willing to ruin the reputations of other writers and throw herself at men in power just to boost her career?

But that's where the memories stopped. She didn't know. She couldn't recall what had triggered her to become a woman she was now ashamed of. She couldn't remember much after she had started writing except that, evidently, she wanted to be the most successful romance writer in the business and the easiest way to accomplish that goal was to persuade herself to do despicable things.

Edith stopped reading and glanced up at Tia. "What is it?"

"I remember. I remember my past. At least most of it. My father hated me and left when I was young, and my mother worked hard to keep us fed. I remember wanting to write to make money to pay her back, but something changed. Somewhere along the way, I stopped caring about my mother and began only caring about myself." Shame filled her. Even though she couldn't remember every event, she knew there would be many she would regret when they surfaced in her memory.

"Fame can do that to people," Edith said.

"But I don't want to be that person any more. I want to go back to the girl who wanted to help her mother."

"Then do it. You control what you do, and it appears you've been given a second chance at your life."

"Oh, I'm sorry. I didn't know you had a guest. I can come back later."

Tia looked up to see an unfamiliar nurse in her doorway. She was slim with olive skin and dark hair. Had Brody reassigned Valerie then?

"It's no bother. You come do what you

have to do. I can read around your examination," Edith said as she glanced briefly at the nurse before dropping her gaze back to her book.

"Um, okay. How is your pain today?" the nurse asked.

"It's better," Tia said, "but shouldn't you be writing that down?" She found it odd that this woman didn't have the clipboard that Valerie and Brody usually walked in with.

The woman's eyes widened, and her gaze flitted around the room. "You're right. I must have forgotten it. It's my first week. I'll go get it and return later."

Tia watched the woman walk out of the room and wondered about her. Was she really new? Forgetting to bring in the clipboard seemed like a ridiculous error even for someone who was new. Perhaps she was affiliated with the people after Tia. Maybe she was disguising herself as a nurse, so she could take Tia out without suspicion. Tia shook her head. Her imagination was running away with her. Things like that only happened in movies or television, but perhaps if she couldn't remember how to write romances, she could write thrillers.

"They really need to train these nurses

better," Edith said when the woman was gone. "She's the same one who tried to run me out yesterday. I told Dr. Cavanaugh he needed to talk to her. Guess I need to remind him again."

The topic of Dr. Cavanaugh distracted Tia from her runaway thoughts of killers in disguise and she found herself asking a question she didn't dare ask anyone else. "Do you know Dr. Cavanaugh well?"

"As well as you can know a doctor I guess," Edith said as her eyes returned to the book. "I read a lot to his wife during her last days."

"What was she like?" Tia had an image of Dr. Cavanaugh's wife in her head, and she wanted to know if the woman was as saintly as she pictured her.

Edith looked up at Tia with a scrutinizing gaze. "She was lovely. A real woman of God. Even when the cancer took hold of her, she always remained positive and friendly to everyone. Now, should I continue reading?"

Tia nodded, but her mind no longer listened as Edith continued reading. She had wandered through the past long enough for today. Now, she needed to figure out how to change her future.

"I HEAR you took your patient outside," Nick said as he came up behind Brody in the locker room.

Brody shrugged, but he was curious who had ratted him out. "It's not against the rules."

Nick opened his locker and pulled out his bag. "No, it's not, but it's not something doctors normally do. It's also very unlike Brody Cavanaugh who never dates and rarely looks at women. And it has the nurses in a fit. You know how they like to gossip."

Brody hung his coat up in the locker. "They gossip about everything. I doubt I'll be the topic of their gossip much longer. Some episode of a tv drama will have replaced me by tomorrow."

"Mmmhmm, but I thought you said you weren't falling for this girl."

Brody sighed and sank down on the bench seat that filled the wall on the other side of the small locker room. He dropped his head into his hands. "I wasn't, but I have to be honest that I am having a hard time getting her off my mind. Every moment I spend with her is....calming, if that makes any sense."

"It makes perfect sense," Nick said as he sat beside Brody. "Look man, I didn't know Rachel well, but I have to think that she wouldn't want this life for you. This throwing yourself into work and never having a social life. From what I did know of her, she would have wanted you to keep living, and part of living is not being alone. So, if you're not pursuing this woman simply because of Rachel…." he shrugged, "I think you're wrong."

"Maybe." Brody shook his head. "But she's also a patient who doesn't remember who she is. And someone is clearly after her. *And* the little I have found out about her past doesn't paint her in the best light."

"Maybe, she just needs something or someone," Nick looked at him pointedly, "to have a reason to change."

Brody smiled up at his friend. "I'll take that into consideration, and I'll think about it. Right now, I better get to the store though. My refrigerator is going to sue me for lack of support." He grabbed his bag and headed for the door.

"That's why you need a Berta," Nick hollered after him. "I'll send you her number."

Brody was still chuckling as he pushed the back door open and found Jordan Graves leaning against his car. "Detective, did you find out anything more about the flowers?"

Jordan pushed himself upright and glanced around the empty lot. "Unfortunately not. They were purchased at the gift shop here, but paid for in cash. The clerk couldn't remember who purchased them and there's no camera that points that direction. We do have some new intel though. It appears Rico Rearden may be involved in drug trafficking over in Chicago. He didn't come up on our initial radar because he doesn't deal here, but it looks like he might hold meetings here and use his publishing business as a front."

"Do you think Tia was helping him move drugs?" Just when Brody thought maybe he could fall for this girl another piece of information rocked his heart. He had a hard-enough time imagining her sleeping with another woman's husband, but moving drugs?

"We don't know what to think. It's possible she was involved though nothing in her background suggests it. It's more probable she was there for the meeting she had scheduled and may have stumbled across a secret meeting. Either way, we need to keep a close eye on her. She may not be as innocent as we think."

Brody shook his head. He'd had no idea one patient would turn his life upside down so fast. "Okay, thanks Jordan, I'll do my best." He shook Jordan's hand and then unlocked the car and slid into the driver's seat. But he didn't start the car right away. His thoughts were a tangled web and he wanted to clear them before he started driving.

Tia Sweetchild certainly was a conundrum. His first assumption of her had been a snobby rich girl, but that image had softened as he'd spent time with her. Her past showed that she had deliberately tried to ruin someone's career, but she had acted appalled when he'd told her about it. Was she a good con or had the brain injury changed her personality? Now there was the possibility of drugs? He didn't want it to believe it. He felt an attraction to Tia. A connection he couldn't explain, but how could he be attracted to a woman with such a shady past?

Rachel had been nothing like that. She'd grown up in a Christian home, and he was pretty sure the champagne they had on their wedding night had been her first taste of alcohol. Curse words never crossed her lips, and she always scolded Brody when he let one slip. And she'd been a genuine, generous, faithful woman. She would never have pursued men to get ahead no matter the circumstances. So, why would he feel an attraction to someone so unlike the love of his life? Or was there more to Tia than he knew?

He had no answers, and with a sigh, he turned the key and pointed the car towards home. Maybe some time in the word and a decent night's sleep would give him some clarity.

CHAPTER 9

$\mathcal{T}$ia glanced with dread at the doorway every time she heard footsteps. She wasn't looking forward to seeing Dr. Cavanaugh this morning. What she had remembered of her past was too shameful, and she was sure she wouldn't be able to hide the shame from him. Maybe it was his day off, and she wouldn't have to face him today.

"Good morning, Tia. Did Detective Graves stop in to see you yesterday?" And there he was.

Tia nodded. "He did though he said the flowers were a dead end. No way to trace who bought them. The security guard is supposed to intercept any from now on."

"Probably a good idea. I'm sorry he wasn't able to obtain more information about the flowers, but how are you feeling today?"

She forced her lips into a smile she didn't feel and hoped he wouldn't notice the difference. "Physically? Not too bad. The ache in my head is down to a dull roar and the throbbing in my foot has intensified which I guess is good because it means I'm feeling it more."

Dr. Cavanaugh nodded and made some notes in the chart. "Pain is rarely fun, but it does sometimes serve a good purpose. And as much as I don't want you in pain, I am glad to hear you have more feeling. I'll schedule a follow up with Dr. North." He lowered the clipboard and regarded her. "Now, how about emotionally?"

Tia scoffed softly and bit the inside of her lip. "Okay, I guess. Edith read some more of this book you brought me, and I remembered a little more of my past."

"That's great," Dr. Cavanaugh said with a smile and what sounded to Tia like a false cheeriness in his voice.

Tia wished it were. Yes, she had remembered some good things about her past, but she also knew somewhere along the way she had changed into an unlikeable person, and she still didn't know exactly why. Nor did she want to share that detail with Dr. Cavanaugh.

He started his daily assessment of her by checking her IV and the monitor that beeped constantly next to her bed. Then his fingers were on her forehead as he checked her stitches. "This is healing nicely. I bet the scar won't be too noticeable."

Tia was fairly certain that a scar of any kind would have sent her over the edge at one point, but now she felt as if she deserved it. And maybe more.

"Your fever appears to be gone as well. We might be able to get you out of here sooner than I thought."

Tia wasn't sure how she felt about that. She certainly hadn't planned on living in this hospital, but she still had no idea where she was staying or who was after her. What would she do when she was released? And would she ever see Dr. Cavanaugh again? Maybe he would be glad to get her out of the hospital.

He had just moved the blanket from her feet when the intercom sounded. "Attention personnel. This is a code silver. I repeat we have a code silver in the ICU."

Dr. Cavanaugh's hands froze and Tia felt a string of fear grip her heart. "What's a code silver?" she asked in a frightened whisper.

"It means someone has a weapon. Stay calm. I'm going to lock the door." He shut her door, locked it, and then began scooting a chair up against the door. When that was in place, he returned to Tia's side.

"This isn't going to feel good, but I need to move you."

"What? Why? What's happening out there?" Panic filled Tia's voice.

"I don't know, but Detective Graves told me yesterday that Rico Rearden is involved with drug trafficking. Now, it's possible you were helping or you stumbled into a meeting you weren't supposed to. Or maybe that weapon has nothing to do with you, but I don't want to take the chance. I've locked the door which will hold them for a bit and I'm certain the security guard will defend the room, but you're a sitting duck in the bed. If I can get you into the bathroom, it buys us a little more time and hopefully it will be enough."

"And if it's not?" It was not a question she needed an answer to, but he gave one anyway.

"Then I hope you're prepared to meet your maker." He held her gaze for just a moment before snapping back to the task at hand. "If you can grab that pole, I can leave the IV in, but I'm going to have to pick you up."

A million thoughts raced through Tia's head. She hadn't had her sponge bath today, he would touch her bare back, if she didn't allow him to pick her up then they could die. "Okay."

As he snaked his arms under her head and knees, she reached for the pole. "Not yet," he said grunting with the effort of lifting her. "I need to get around the bed first."

Tia wrapped a free arm around his neck in hopes it might lessen his load and grimaced against the pain as her foot fell below her heart. The throbbing intensified, but she pressed her lips together to keep from complaining. He was doing the hard work here, and she would not whine.

When they cleared the bed, he took a step toward the IV drip and she grabbed the pole. The wheels squeaked softly as they made their way across the floor and Tia hoped the sound wasn't carrying outside the room. An eerie silence filled the air.

When they reached the bathroom, he set her down in the tub as gingerly as he could. The pain from her foot made the world go black for a moment, but then he was propping her foot up with towels from the shelf. Once it was above her heart again, the pain lessened and the blackness receded.

"I hope you aren't afraid of the dark," he said as he pulled the door shut and locked it.

Tia wasn't normally afraid of the darkness, but she'd long hated darkness if mirrors were involved. A silly childhood game had planted an absurd fear of nightmarish things coming out of mirrors in the dark, and though she'd realized as she grew older that the game was just that, her fear hadn't diminished. Though she couldn't see him, she was glad Dr. Cavanaugh was in the room with her.

BRODY TRIED to calm his breath as he pulled his phone out of his pocket. He punched in Jordan's number and hoped he would get bars. The reception in the hospital was spotty enough in the break room, but he'd never tried it in a bathroom. He pressed the call button and watched as the phone searched for a connection. "Please God," he whispered. A moment later, two bars appeared. It wasn't much, but he hoped it would be enough. He held his breath as he waited.

"Detective Graves," the voice on the other end said as his call went through.

"Jordan? It's Brody Cavanaugh at Fire Beach Hospital. We are in lockdown. A code silver was reported a few moments ago in the ICU. I am locked in the bathroom in room six with Tia." Brody was surprised at how calm his voice sounded as his heart pounded in his chest.

"I'm on my way. Do you know what the weapon is?"

"No, I haven't seen anything. I locked the door per protocol as soon as the announcement was made."

"Understood. I'm going to transfer you to a dispatch operator and I want you to stay on the line until I get there."

"I'll try, but we're in the bathroom and I only had two bars. I don't know if they'll hold..... Hello?" He pulled the phone away from his ear and sighed as he saw it searching for connection again. At least the bars had been there long enough for him to place the call. The rest was in God's hands now.

He turned toward the bathtub. "Tia, how are you holding up?"

"Okay, I think. The throbbing has subsided in my foot."

Brody reached out a hand hoping it would land on her arm and not some other body part. He felt the flesh of her bare skin and a moment later, her hand covered his.

"Are you scared?" she asked in a timid voice.

He interlocked his fingers with hers. "A little. You?"

"Yeah. A lot. Do you think the police will make it in time Dr. Cavanaugh?"

Brody shook his head though he knew she couldn't see it in the darkness. "I hope so. Tia?"

"Yeah?"

"I think considering the circumstances that you can call me Brody."

He could hear the smile in her voice even though it was laced by fear. "Okay, Brody." She squeezed his hand, and he liked how his name sounded on her lips. "Can I ask you something?"

Brody didn't think their voices would carry out of the bathroom, especially in the hushed whispers they were using and talking sounded a lot better than sitting in silence and worrying if someone would bust in and end their lives. "Sure, ask away."

Her deep breath sounded nearly deafening in the dark silence. "How did you know you wanted to be a doctor?"

"Oh, um." No one had asked him that question in a long time. He thought back over the years and smiled as he recalled his childhood. "My mother said I always enjoyed pretending to heal animals and people when I was young, but I think the first time I knew I wanted to become a doctor was in high school. There was a student with epilepsy and one day she had a grand mal seizure in class. I remember everyone being so scared, even the teacher, and I wished I knew what to do to help her. After that, I began researching what it would take to become a doctor and never turned back. What about you? Do you remember why you became a writer?"

Her voice was barely above a whisper as it came back to him. "I do. I remembered yesterday that my father left us. He never wanted me. He said he wanted a boy, but I'm not sure he really wanted a kid at all. Before I could write, I used to make up stories to escape his anger, but after he left, I began writing stories of the family I wished I had. I wanted it to be a career, so I could support my mother and repay her for all she did."

Brody's heart broke with her words. Fathers were so important, and in this age where families broke apart and men encouraged their wives and girlfriends to have abortions, good father figures were harder and harder to find. He'd been lucky. Not only were his parents still together, but his father had always been there for him.

"I'm so sorry, Tia. I can't imagine how hard that must have been." Though he didn't condone some of her past behavior, this admission could explain why she had done some of the things she had. If she had become so focused on making enough money to help her mother, greed might have taken control of the once sweet girl and changed her into the woman who would throw another person under the bus to further her career.

"Me too." Another long sigh. "Can I ask you something else?"

"Go ahead." Talking broke the heavy

silence, and he didn't think she could ask him anything he might not want to answer.

"Do you think you'll ever marry again, Brody?"

Except that! He bit the inside of his lip as he thought of how to answer.

Brody. The name felt like candy on her tongue. How she would have enjoyed this moment of holding his hand and saying his name if it weren't clouded with the darkness and fear around them.

Darkness and fear.... Suddenly, the events of a few nights ago came back to her. She saw herself entering Rico's house and following him to his bedroom. While sleeping with him hadn't been her plan, she had been prepared to use flirtation and her good looks on him to try and get her book promoted. At least until she saw the picture of his wife on the nightstand. "Oh my gosh, Brody, I remember." She squeezed his hand tighter as excitement joined the fear coursing through her.

"What?" he asked.

"I went to Rico's to try and convince him to promote my latest book, but I didn't know about his wife. When I realized he was married, I told him I wouldn't cross that line. I've been pretty awful the last few years but that was too much for even me. But as we were talking, his phone rang. His demeanor shifted immediately, and he ushered me out of the room. I was almost to my car when I remembered my purse. I ran back up to his room, but he freaked out when he saw me and shoved me in a closet." She shivered as she remembered sitting in the unfamiliar dark closet.

"I thought he was hiding me from his wife, but then I heard other masculine voices join his. They were angry and yelling about something, but the words were muffled inside the closet. Anyway, I heard the balcony glass door open, and I took the chance they had stepped outside. I bolted, forgetting my purse in the process. I just wanted to get out of there."

"Do you think they were in the black truck that hit you?" Brody asked.

"It's possible. I never saw the driver, but I remember one car blinding me from behind and then the truck hitting me. If it was them, I don't think they'll stop until I'm dead."

Her words hung in the air, a fatal prophecy. Neither of them had a word to say in response. Suddenly, there was a pounding on the door of her hospital room. Tia squeezed Brody's hand tighter. "Brody? If we don't make it out of here alive, I want you to know that I'm glad you were my doctor. You're a good man, and you've made me want to be a better woman."

"Shh, don't talk like that," Brody said, but the fear was evident in his voice.

Suddenly, there was pounding on the bathroom door. Tia squeezed Brody's hand tighter with one hand and clapped the other over her mouth to keep from screaming.

"Dr. Cavanaugh? Open up. It's Detective Graves."

Relief flooded Tia and her breath escaped in one giant sigh. Even when Brody let go of her hand to stand and open the door, she had never felt so blissful. The bright light blinded her for a moment, and she blinked rapidly to readjust her eyes.

"Is it safe to come out then?" Brody asked.

"It is," Detective Graves said, "Evidently, it was a patient who suffered a psychiatric break and grabbed a scalpel off a tray."

Tia might have laughed at the situation if her heartbeat wasn't still thundering in her chest.

"I'm sorry," Brody said, "after our conversation-"

"You were right to do what you did," Detective Graves assured him. "We still haven't found the driver of the black truck or who sent her those flowers and what you did made perfect sense. However, unless you need further assistance, we'll get back to work on finding the suspects."

"Wait Detective Graves?" Though Tia didn't want to recount her story again, she didn't want another reprimand from Detective Graves either. He turned back to her and waited for her to continue. "I remembered more. I was there to see Rico about a publishing opportunity, but I turned it down when I found out he was married and looking for an affair. He kicked me out, but I had forgotten my purse. When I returned, he shoved me in a closet. I heard men's voices arguing, and I thought perhaps they were reporters out for a story on me which is why I ran when I did."

"Did you see any of the men? Do you remember anything about them?"

"Not their faces. When I stepped out of the closet, I looked left. They were on the balcony, but it was dark outside. I couldn't see their faces, but I felt the icy hatred in their gaze when they saw me. I didn't think they had followed me at first, but then lights blinded me on the road. I slowed down thinking maybe it was just teenagers out for a joy ride, but when they didn't pass me, I figured they had followed me after all. Then the truck hit me."

Jordan's face hardened and he exchanged a glance with Brody. "Okay, thank you, Tia. We'll look into all of this and let you know what we find. Do the two of you need anything else?"

"I think we'll be fine." Brody turned to Tia as the detectives left. "Well, that was some excitement for the day. How about we get you back in bed?"

"Could we take a walk instead?" Tia asked. "My heart is still pounding, and I feel like I could use some fresh air after this."

His lips pulled into a smile. "I think that's a great idea."

※

BRODY TRIED to ignore the sensations that flooded his body when he picked Tia up again. He'd been sure there was no emotional attachment or he'd at least been trying to convince himself there was no attachment, but the near-death experience had blown that out of the water. Holding hands with her in the dark had sent emotions careening through his body that he hadn't felt since Rachel's death.

But he still didn't know her. Was she the overly ambitious, conniving person of her past? She said she hadn't had an affair or involvement with drug trafficking. But was that true? Or was she the sweet, kind person that he knew her to be? He had to admit that even though he didn't completely know her, the things in her past seemed to matter less now. She seemed sincere.

"Let me get you a robe," he said as soon as he got her situated back on the bed. He grabbed one from the wardrobe in the room and helped her shrug into it before paging for a wheelchair. Then he looked at her, a million things running through his mind – none of which he could say. "I'll check your IV."

"You've taken very good care of me, Brody. Thank you," Tia said holding his gaze.

He liked how his name sounded when she said it. And he liked taking care of her. Egad, was he falling for her?

"Dr. Cavanaugh? Your wheelchair."

The sound of the orderly snapped Brody out of his daydream and he flashed Eric a smile. "Thank you. Can you let Valerie know I'm taking a walk?"

Eric paled. "I will, sir, but you should know they are talking about you. About how much time you're spending..." he glanced over at Tia, "with patients."

"That's all right, Eric. I can handle it, but thank you for the information." Brody didn't like being the subject of gossip, but he hadn't been exaggerating when he told Nick they gossiped about everything. He wasn't about to change his behavior just to avoid being their topic.

"Can we go without the pole?" Tia asked. She had either not caught Eric's implication or she was simply ignoring it.

"If you think you can handle no pain meds for a bit, I can cap your plug."

"I think I'll be okay. Honestly, the pain is getting better. Of course, that could be the medicine talking." She flashed him a crooked smile, "or maybe the adrenaline. But really, I think I'll be fine for the walk."

He pushed up the sleeve of her robe and unhooked the IV, being careful to leave the plug in her arm. Then he wheeled the chair closer to the bed and helped her sit down. Moments later, they were outside breathing in the sunlight and fresh air.

"You know for a minute, I thought that might be the end," Tia said as he pushed her down the path. She had suggested they walk this time instead of just sitting, and after the scare, Brody was in need of some exercise to settle his nerves as well. "I realized I don't want this to be the end of my life. Whether this personality change is because of me or the brain injury, I want to do something with it. I want to apologize to Ava and the other people I have hurt and start walking a different path."

"I think that's a great plan," Brody said with a smile as he imagined helping her accomplish that goal. But then he remembered she lived in California and he lived here. "Will you go back to California then?"

"I don't know," she said. "I mean I guess I will have to go back to check the details of my life there, but I might like it here. Or I might when people aren't trying to kill me."

"Yeah, that could prevent someone from liking a place," Brody chuckled.

"You know, you never answered my question."

"What question?" In all the commotion of her memory coming back and the rescue, he had forgotten what she had asked.

"Do you think you'll ever marry again?"

Brody was glad he was behind her and she couldn't see his facial expressions because he had no idea what emotion might be playing on his face right now. "I don't know. When Rachel died, I was pretty sure that was it. I threw myself into work and convinced myself it would be enough, but now I'm not so sure. I suppose I'd like a companion again. If I could find the right woman."

She smiled up at him, and Brody felt the ice around his heart melt a little more. Though he hadn't expected it to happen, she had managed to capture a piece of his heart.

"Well, I hope you do then. You seem like you would make a great husband."

Brody didn't know what to say to that, so they continued on in silence. They walked around the entire hospital enjoying the sun and fresh air.

"Oh, I never thanked you," she said as they reached the entrance again.

"For what?" he asked.

"For reassigning Valerie. The new nurse is much nicer though I feel like she might need more training. She forgot the clipboard when she came in to check me."

Brody felt a tendril of fear reach around his heart and begin to squeeze. "Tia, I didn't assign a new nurse to your room."

She turned to face him, panic in her eyes. "Then who is the nurse who was in my room yesterday?"

"I don't know, but we better find out." Brody's shoulders, having just relaxed, tensed again, and he pulled out his cell phone to dial Jordan once again as he wheeled Tia back inside.

CHAPTER 11

Tia flipped on the television to pass the time before Brody's return. Her heart still thudded faster than normal in her chest. When they had returned to the room, Brody and Jordan had gone in search of the nurse she had seen yesterday. Jordan had left strict instructions with the security guard outside that no one was allowed in her room except Sophie, but that thought didn't make her feel much safer. What if the security guard fell asleep or was overpowered or went to the bathroom for goodness sake?

She wished Brody had stayed with her. It wasn't even evening yet, but the day had been more eventful than most. More eventful than she thought her life back home ever was. In fact, though she still didn't remember everything, when she thought of her life back home, she only felt loneliness. Did she really want to go back to that?

"Reflecting on your poor choices?'"

Tia's eyes flicked to the doorway and she sucked in her breath. A man she did not recognize stood in the doorway dressed in an orderly uniform. Except for the ice flowing out of his gaze and the hard lines of his face, he might have been any orderly in the hospital, but she knew he was not. Fear raced through her. "How did you get in here?" she asked as she inched her finger toward the call button.

"I wouldn't do that if I were you." He let go of the door and lunged toward her with a vicious scowl. The door shut behind him, and the movement caused Tia to jump and her hand slipped away from the call button. "You want to know how I got past your security guard?"

Tia nodded, fear constricting her voice.

He flashed a cold, predatory smile. "I just gave him a little something to help him sleep. The same thing I'm going to do to you. See, Rico's wife came in guns blazing, the idiot, but I'm smarter than that. I think things through. I gather all the information, and I don't make mistakes."

"Who are you and why are you doing this?" Tia asked hoping to stall him. "I didn't hear the conversation and wouldn't have remembered it if I had. And I never saw your face. Until now. You could have just let it go. Let me go."

He shook his head as his lips pulled into a chilling smile. "Who I am is unimportant. At least to you, but you? You're a loose end. I don't like loose ends." He pulled a syringe from his pocket. "Do you know what this is?"

"No, but I bet you're going to tell me." Tia's eyes darted to the door hoping for someone, anyone to walk in. Brody had no reason to return so soon, but maybe Valerie? As much as she didn't like the nurse, she would welcome her presence right now.

"It's insulin." He took another step toward her. "Do you know what happens when you get injected with insulin too quickly and you're not diabetic?"

"I'm sure nothing good." Tia's heart pounded in her chest. Should she scream? Would anyone hear her through the closed door? Maybe she could try for the button again, but she wasn't sure this man didn't have another weapon. Would he just pull out a gun and shoot her if she tried?

"First, it will make you groggy and confused before you pass out completely. The damage to your organs will be done before they even know what happened, and the best part is that insulin is already in the body, so nobody will think twice if they find it. They'll probably assume you just had a delayed traumatic reaction to today's events."

Panic squeezed on her heart, but she forced herself to keep him talking. "Did you have something to do with the code silver?"

Something akin to pride filled his face. "I may have helped a patient secure a scalpel and then prodded them in the right direction. It would have been the perfect time to silence you, especially since your security guard was tasked to help, but I wasn't counting on your doctor being in the room." Anger replaced the pride for a moment and transformed his face into an expression of rage.

"I thought you didn't make mistakes." What was wrong with her? Why was she goading him on? Did she really think she was buying enough time for someone to come to her rescue?

"Hmm," he chuckled, but it was a cold,

calculating laugh. "See? I knew you listened, and now it's time to rectify that mistake."

As he lunged toward her, Tia did the only thing she could. She opened her mouth and screamed.

As THE DARK-HAIRED nurse caught sight of them, she ran. Jordan bolted after her, turning his head just long enough to order Brody back to Tia's room. Then, he disappeared around the corner as well.

Brody hurried back to the ICU floor. He had just reached the center desk when he heard the noise. He wasn't sure it was a scream, but the sound of it sent the hairs on the back of his neck standing at attention. He glanced around at the few nurses who were in the ICU with him. "What was that?" Then his eyes darted to Tia's room. Her door was shut which was unusual, and the security guard was slumped in the chair outside. "Call security," he hollered as he raced across the floor to her room.

He checked the pulse of the security guard first. Weak, but still there. He didn't know for how long. "Someone get this man some help," he ordered and then, without a second thought to his own safety, he burst through the door in time to see an orderly inject something into her IV. "What are you doing?"

The man looked up at him, and the expression chilled Brody to the bone. His eyes were hard and cruel as if chiseled from stone, and there was not a shred of remorse or decency in them. "You don't work here. Get away from her." Brody glanced to Tia whose eyes were beginning to close. What had he injected her with? He had to find out soon or he might not be able to counter it.

"Gladly," the man said, "my job here is done anyway." He began to skirt around the bed, but Brody had no intentions of letting him get out of the room. For every step he made, Brody countered. "Out of my way," the man snarled.

Brody had taken some self-defense classes in college and he had done some kickboxing. But fighting someone was an experience he had never had before. "I don't think so. The police are on their way. I think you'll be staying here until they arrive." He stepped into the fighter's stance his muscles remembered - left foot forward, hands at the ready by his chin.

The man chuckled. "You want to fight me?"

"If that's what it takes to see you arrested, I will."

"You're no match for me." He reached into his pocket and pulled out a knife.

Brody had never fought anyone with a knife and images of previous stab victims bleeding out on his ER tables flashed through his mind, but he wasn't going to give up. Surely, he could last until security or Jordan arrived.

The man lunged for him and Brody stepped to the side and threw a left hook. He missed the man's chin, but his fist hit the man's face with enough force to cause him to stumble forward. Brody took the opportunity to deliver a low kick to the back of the man's knee and he went sprawling. The knife skidded away. With an angry roar, the man lunged at Brody and threw him into the wall. Brody hit the sharp corner where the bathroom jutted out and felt the pain race down his left side, but he didn't have time to dwell on it long before the man was on top of him. His powerful hands closed on

Brody's throat and the world began to go dark.

And then there was air. Brody opened his eyes to see security hauling the man out of the room, but his head was still spinning from the momentary lack of oxygen.

"Are you okay?" Valerie's face appeared above him.

"Tia," he croaked and coughed. "He injected her with something. Probably insulin. Get her some Glycogen. The security guard outside too."

Valerie looked as if she wanted to argue, but she nodded and raced over to the bed. Brody reached a hand up to massage his neck. He'd been lucky, and he knew it. When he could take a solid breath, he pushed himself to a sitting position and then stood pausing only long enough to make sure the world wasn't spinning before racing to Tia's side.

Valerie stepped back from the IV and then hurried out of the room to administer one to the security guard. Brody stared down at Tia. Suddenly, her eyes fluttered open and she blinked. Then her gaze locked on Brody, and she gripped his arm. "Did he escape?" Fear threaded Tia's voice and her eyes shifted to the doorway.

"No, security got him."

"But not before he got Dr. Cavanaugh," Valerie said pointedly as she re-entered the room. "You need to get checked out yourself."

"I will," Brody said. In addition to a pounding in his head, he could feel the left side of his body stiffening. "But not until I talk to Detective Graves."

CHAPTER 12

ia found it nearly impossible to relax even with Brody sitting beside her. Every sound made her jump and look to the doorway.

"It's going to be all right," Brody said as he held out a hand. She was grateful for his touch, but even that didn't calm her racing heart. In just a few days, she'd been in an automobile accident, had a gun pulled on her, been locked in a bathroom due to a code silver, and been injected with Insulin. She wasn't sure her heart would ever return to its normal rhythm.

"How are you two doing?"

Tia looked up to see Detective Graves in the doorway.

"Did you get the guy?" Brody asked. "Who was he?"

Detective Graves nodded. "We did. His name is Adrian Petrov. He's the leader of one of the bigger gangs out of Chicago and the head of a drug organization. He isn't saying much right now, but Stone will take care of that. We did manage to ascertain his address." He turned to Tia and a slight smile pulled at his lips, "Where we found a black Ford truck, and though he tried to have it fixed, we are almost certain it was the same truck that hit you. It's over, Tia."

"That's wonderful." Brody turned to Tia, and a broad grin graced his features.

Tia forced a smile in return, but her worry wasn't entirely eased. She didn't know why, but the situation still bothered her. "Wait, what about the nurse?"

"We got her too. Susanna Petrov, his wife. She's not talking either, but from what we can gather, they obtained uniforms when they saw on the news that you were in ICU. We're not sure whether she was merely keeping him informed or if she was a backup plan, but we do know that she's the one who bought the flowers. We showed pictures to the clerk at the gift shop, and he was able to ID her."

So that was it. It was over, except.... "What about Rico?" Where did he fit into all of this? Why hadn't he come after her?

Jordan's jaw clenched and his eyes shifted just slightly. "He's in the wind. We think he's in Chicago hiding out and trying to clean up this mess, but I promise you, we're still looking for him."

It should make her feel better, but it didn't. "Thank you, Detective Graves."

"Call me Jordan," he said as he held her gaze.

"Yes, thank you, Jordan," Brody said clapping a hand on Jordan's shoulder before turning back to Tia. "We need to monitor you to be sure the insulin didn't damage anything, but if all goes well, and as long as your fever is still gone, you might be able to leave the hospital tomorrow."

She should be glad. No one wanted to live in a hospital, but Tia didn't know what life held for her now. Did she go back to writing? She wasn't sure her stories would be the same after everything that had happened, and she didn't want to chance falling into the person she had been before. But, if she didn't write, what would she do?

As if sensing her unease, Detective Graves

stepped forward. "I know this is a lot to deal with, Tia. If you'd like to stay in town a little longer, I can find you a temporary place and set you up with a counselor who might be able to work through some of the trauma with you."

Tia smiled up at him. "Thank you, I might take you up on that."

"And I don't know how your recovery will be, but I own a restaurant. I have a need for a good hostess if your doctor says it's okay."

Brody nodded. "I'd be okay with it as long as she can stay off her leg. It would be great if you stayed in town, and I was able to check up on you as well."

Check up on her? Was that all he wanted? She had thought after their two near death experiences that he might want more, but perhaps that had just been adrenaline acting and not any real affection for her.

"Thank you, Jordan. I think I'll spend tonight thinking about where I see my life going from here, and I'll let you know."

"You do that." He pulled a card from his pocket and handed it to her. "I know Al gave you a card the first day we were here, but this one has my personal cell. You call me if you want some help. I'm sorry this happened to you, but you are strong. You will be okay."

Tia nodded and hoped her lips formed a smile though she didn't feel much like smiling. After Jordan left, Brody went to check on other patients, promising to check in on her before he left for the night.

As she lay in the quiet room, Tia wondered what the rest of her life held for her. If Brody didn't have feelings for her, would she stay in Fire Beach? There wouldn't really be a need, but could she readjust to her life back in California? It already felt a lifetime ago. Though she couldn't remember the last time she had, Tia turned her eyes to the ceiling and whispered a prayer.

"God? I don't know if I used to do this. I'm not even sure I'm doing it right, but if I am, please help me know what to do. I don't want to go back to the person I was before, but I have no idea how to go forward."

She hadn't expected a booming answer, but Tia sighed when all she received was the stillness of her room broken only by the beeping of her monitor.

"WHEW, YOU TOOK QUITE A POUNDING," Nick said as he helped Brody get his arm out of the shirt. Though he didn't think anything was broken, Brody wanted to get a second opinion before heading home for the night. Besides worker's compensation required he receive medical attention for his claim.

Brody tried not to grimace as the pain shot through him. His arm was already turning an ugly collection of blue and purples. "I know, but it was either take the guy down or let him get away."

"In that case, I think you chose wisely, but you should remember that you're not Superman. You're going to have a sizable bruise on this shoulder. I'd ice it tonight and think about taking a few days off to recover. You certainly have enough saved up."

"Yeah, maybe after Tia gets released," Brody said with a nod. He tried to lift his arm to replace his shirt, but the pain made him stop.

Nick stepped back and narrowed his eyes at Brody. "Tia, huh? You've saved this woman twice now, and you don't want to take time off while she's here. Are you really going to tell me you don't have feelings for this woman?"

Brody sighed. "I don't know what I have - whether it's feelings or some crazy case of needing to protect her, but I want to be here until she's released."

"You don't even know how bad you have it, man," Nick said with a shake of his head as he helped Brody place his arm back in his sleeves. "Okay, let me see the hip."

Brody took a deep breath, stood, and lowered his pants. His hip was definitely sore and would probably be just as colorful, but his shoulder actually ached more.

"Yep, you're going to have fun walking the next few days. Ice and rest, man. Ice and rest. And no more fist fights or wall slams."

"I'll do my best," Brody said with a smirk. "It's not like I practice them on a regular basis." He zipped his pants back up and grabbed his bag. "Thanks, Nick. I'll see you tomorrow."

"You too. Oh, and Brody?" Brody turned back to his friend. "She won't be your patient much longer."

Brody smiled and flashed his friend a wave as he stepped out of the door. Was that his hang-up? Was he worried about how it would look if he were seeing a patient? He supposed it was possible. There was no denying he had feelings for Tia now, but were they worth pursuing? Would she return to California when she was released? He had so many questions and no real answers. Perhaps tomorrow would bring more clarity.

CHAPTER 13

Tia's eyes snapped open at the sound of footsteps. Her room was dark, too dark. It was night, so it had to have just been a nurse, but why wouldn't they identify themselves? She blinked trying to adjust to the light level and held her breath to hear any sounds better. But there was nothing. Had it all been a dream then? It had seemed so real.

As she exhaled, she wondered if she would face this the rest of her life. Would she always be jumping at shadows and feeling like she was being watched? Jordan had said it was over, but what if it wasn't? What if someone was still out there? What if Rico came after her? What if there were more people involved in the meeting than who Jordan arrested? Would she ever be safe?

She was still tired when the sun woke her the next morning. That certainly hadn't been her best night of sleep, and the responsibilities of the upcoming day wore heavy on her. If she got released, she needed to find a place to stay at least until her foot healed. Though Brody had said she could fly, trying to maneuver travel with a cast didn't sound appealing at all. Besides, she was in no hurry to get back to her life. Plus, she would need to contact Jordan about his job offer. Tia hoped to return to writing one day, but until she got back on her feet, she needed a job that provided consistent income.

"Are you ready for your final evaluation?" Brody asked entering the room.

"I should say yes, right?"

"Most people can't wait to leave though I think it's mostly to get better food," he said with a smile.

"Well most people don't have people trying to kill them either."

"Did something happen?" Brody's voice oozed with concern and his eyes raked over her as if looking for injuries. "Jordan said it was over."

Tia shook her head. "Just a dream. I know he said it was over, but I don't feel like it is, and I feel it will be worse out there. I certainly won't have you to protect me." She had meant for the words to sound light - an attempt at humor - but they hung heavy in the air.

Brody set his clipboard down on the table and approached her side. His eyes grew serious as he picked up her hand. "About that, Tia. I'm kind of a mess, and I've probably forgotten how to date, but I can't stand here and say I don't care about you. And as much as I don't know what the future holds, I'd like to see if there's a future for us."

Tia's mouth opened, but she couldn't form the words she wanted to say. She had hoped he felt the same as she did, but he'd been impossible to read accurately.

"I can't promise any more Superman stunts, but I'll try my best to protect you."

"Did you hurt yourself badly?" she finally managed.

"I'll have some good bruising on my left side where I hit that corner," he pointed to the area that jutted out due to the bathroom, "but nothing that won't heal with time. Now, what do you say we get you looked at and get you out of here?"

Tia nodded and chuckled. "I don't think I've ever wanted anything more."

BRODY DECIDED to start at the top and checked Tia's head first. As his fingers touched near her stitches, he couldn't help but wonder how touching the rest of her face would feel. He let his eyes wander down her slender cheek bones and to the curve in her neck before clearing his throat and forcing his focus back to her wound. "This looks good. You ready for the stitches to come out?"

"I suppose." Her eyes flicked up to meet his gaze. "Does it hurt? I don't think I've ever had stitches before."

"Not generally. Most people say it tickles, but I did have a patient once who healed really quickly and her skin grew over her stitches a little."

"Oh great, thanks for sharing that."

He smiled down at her and squeezed her arm for reassurance. "I'm sure that won't be your case. You've had enough issues to deal with." He crossed to the medical cabinet and pulled out a pair of scissors before returning to her side. With a quick snip, he popped the first string holding it all together and then tugged on it until the rest came out. "All done. Did it hurt?"

Tia's face scrunched as if she were deciding. "I guess not, but it didn't tickle either. Is the scar bad?"

Brody pressed around the red puckering to make sure it was holding before answering her. "It's a little red right now, but that's to be expected. It will fade and eventually you'll just have a tiny white line. Besides, scars build character."

"I guess I'll have a lot of character then," she said with a chuckle.

He checked her eye next. The colors had faded to an ugly yellow brown, but she could open it fully, and nothing else appeared to be damaged. The cuts on her face and arms were almost healed as well, so he moved down to check her foot. "Can you feel this?" he asked touching her toes.

Her smile was wide as she nodded. "I can."

"Good, and how about the pain today?"

"Not bad although I assume I don't get to take the good stuff with me when I leave?"

He chuckled as he checked off her progress on the chart. "No, but I'll get you a prescription for some stronger ibuprofen than you can get over-the-counter just in case. I want Dr. North to check your foot as well, but it looks like you're cleared to go unless she says otherwise. You won't be able to drive though. Do you have anyone who can pick you up?"

Her face fell and understanding filled her eyes. "I don't. I don't have a car or a place to live yet."

"Hey, it's okay. I'll call Jordan and see if he can help you out. If he's busy, you can stay here until I get off and I'll drive you wherever he sets up for you."

"Thank you. I promise I won't always be so needy."

He picked up her hand and squeezed it. "We all need people, and I'm happy to help. You just relax and enjoy your last day. I'll take care of the rest."

CHAPTER 14

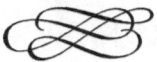

*J*ordan showed up shortly after Dr. North finished her assessment and announced she was cleared to go as well.

"Brody said you could use a lift," he said with a grin. He held a bag in his hands, and she wondered what it contained.

"Yeah, I could. Plus, I thought I'd take you up on your offer for a place to stay and a job. I'd like to stay in town a little longer."

His eyes danced and the corners of his lips twitched as he set the bag beside her on the bed. "Would that have anything to do with a handsome doctor by chance?"

"It might," she said, "but I also don't know if there's much to go back to in

California. I feel like I can start over here except...." Her voice trailed off as she remembered her dream from the previous night.

"Except what?"

Tia sighed and shook her head. "I had a dream last night that someone is still after me. I'm sure it was due to the activity yesterday, but do you think there's any chance that it might be true?"

Jordan ran a hand across his chin. "I'd be lying if I said no. I do think we got the main people involved, but there's always the chance that someone else decides to seek retribution. If it makes you feel better, the lady who runs the house I'm taking you to is former military. She'll keep an eye on you."

"Did you get any news on Rico?"

He shook his head. "Sorry, we're checking with the PD in Chicago, but it's going to take some time."

"Thanks Jordan." She wished that made her feel better, but at least she felt like she had friends looking out for her. Something she didn't think she'd had the last few years.

"You're welcome. Now, in that bag are some clothes and shoes. My girlfriend Cassidy deduced that you had none here. She picked them out, but I had to guess on your size so don't blame her if they're off. She did bring some things with drawstrings so the size shouldn't matter too much."

Tia's fingers touched the bag. Brody was so thoughtful. She hadn't even realized she had no clothes with which to leave the hospital. "Thank you, Jordan, and tell Cassidy thank you."

He nodded, clearly embarrassed and took a step back. "I'll give you a chance to change and see about getting a wheelchair so we can get you out of here."

As he ducked out of the room, Tia opened the bag. Not only did it contain socks and underwear in a few sizes, but there were also stretchy pants and sweats along with a few shirts. As she pulled out a simple green shirt, another piece of her past opened. Back home, she had a large closet full of designer clothes, and she would never have been caught dead in a shirt like this, one that looked as if it came from a bargain store, but Tia found she didn't mind now. Designer clothes seemed insignificant compared to everything she had faced recently.

She pulled on the green shirt and a pair of wide-leg navy stretchy pants, gritting through the pain and stiffness of her body. Then she attempted to put a sock on her left foot, but no matter how hard she tried, she couldn't reach it. She finally decided just to use the sandals Cassidy had provided and forgo the socks altogether.

A knock sounded at the door a few minutes after she finished. "It's Jordan. Can I come in?"

"Yes, come on in."

"Hey, looking good," he said as he wheeled a chair in. Tia wasn't sure she would go that far, but she was thankful for all he had done. "You about ready? I just got called back to work, so I'm afraid I'll have to drop you and run."

"That's fine, Jordan. Really, you've done so much for me."

"So, I took your advice," Brody said as he set his food down across from Nick.

"Oh yeah, about what?" Nick picked up his burger and took a huge bite sending a blob of ketchup down his hand.

Brody rolled his eyes. He loved his friend but sometimes he had the manners of a pig and the memory of a gnat. "About Tia. I've decided to date her and see what happens."

Nick licked the ketchup off his arm. "That's great man. You take my advice about the other stuff too? The icing and time off from work?"

"Yes. Today is my last shift for a week. I'm not sure exactly what I'll do, but I imagine helping Tia get settled will take some of that time." Brody took a bite of his own burger, making sure to hold it over the plate in case he had a similar experience with his ketchup.

"Take her out, man. Fancy dinners, movies, anything that has a ton of people and will keep you both safe. Dancing is probably out for the moment though." Nick chuckled at his own joke before wolfing down another large bite of hamburger.

"You think?" Dancing would probably be out of the question for another few months as would anything requiring both legs, but fancy dinners and movies he could do. He just hoped he remembered how to date. He had met Rachel in college and he'd known from the first date that he was going to marry her. They'd been married for ten years, so his knowledge of dating protocol was definitely rusty.

"It hasn't changed much if that's what you're worried about," Nick said as if reading his mind.

"What?"

"Dating. You had this look on your face - the one you get when you're really thinking about something or about to throw up - so I thought I'd clarify. Just ask the girl to go places with you and have fun. It's still the same."

Brody chuckled and shook his head. "I don't know how you know me so well, Nick. It's kind of creepy."

Nick shrugged and shoved the last of his burger in his mouth. "I'm just that good," he said around his mouthful of food.

Brody smiled as he finished his own lunch. He might not miss this hospital for the next week, but he would miss seeing Nick every day.

CHAPTER 15

ordan parked the car in front of a weathered-looking rambler close to the beach. The yellow paint was faded but still cheery. "Sorry, it's not much to look at on the outside, but Cara takes good care of the inside."

"It's fine," Tia said. "Hopefully, I don't have to inconvenience her too long."

Jordan touched her arm. "It's no inconvenience. We take care of each other here."

Tia smiled and thanked him. She couldn't remember a time she'd had friends like this - friends willing to help her out even though she had brought trouble to town and had a checkered past.

"Come on, I'll introduce you and help you get settled before I jet back to work."

He turned the engine off and walked around to Tia's side. Before helping her out, he grabbed her crutches out of the back seat, handed them to her, and made sure she was stable. Only then did he grab her bag. Tia smiled at his thoughtfulness. She didn't know Cassidy, but she believed the woman had been lucky finding a man like Jordan.

Jordan led the way up the short walk and pushed open the door without knocking. He must know this Cara well. "Cara? It's Jordan and Tia, the woman I told you about."

A woman with short spiky hair appeared in the doorway. Trim and athletic, the woman looked as if she could tangle with the boys any day with her broad shoulders and bold arm definition. "Jordan, good to see you again." She extended a hand in greeting.

Jordan shook the woman's hand and then turned to Tia. "This is Tia. She's recovering from memory loss and a few attempts on her life. She's going to need some help getting back on her feet."

Cara extended her hand to Tia. "It's a pleasure to meet you, and any friend of Jordan's is welcome here as long as needed."

Tia shook the woman's hand and returned the smile. "Thank you. I appreciate it."

"I hate to run, but I have to get to work. Cara will take good care of you, but please call me if you need anything." Jordan squeezed her shoulder before dropping her bag and exiting out the front door.

"Okay, want to follow me and I'll show you to your room?" Cara asked picking up the bag.

Tia nodded and followed her down the hall, her crutches tapping on the wooden floor. Cara stopped in front of a door and opened it to a small room decorated in tan and beige. It held only a bed, nightstand, and dresser, but it was better than the hospital room.

"There's a bathroom right next door. Sorry you'll have to walk a bit to get there, and the dining room is down the hall there. I serve breakfast at seven, lunch at noon, and dinner at seven. If you want a snack during the day, you're welcome to the kitchen."

"Thank you. This is more than I expected," Tia said surprised at the hitch in her voice.

"We've all been there," Cara said and

though she didn't put a hand on Tia's shoulder, she felt the sentiment all the same.

After Cara left, Tia sat on the bed for a moment and looked around. It wasn't home, but it would do. For now.

BRODY PULLED up in front of the house and turned off the car. It appeared weathered and in need of repair on the outside, but Jordan had assured him that Tia would be well taken care of. He planned to help out as much as possible as well.

A blonde woman he had never met before opened the door at his knock. Her features were stern, but kind. "You must be Brody," she said, extending her hand. "I'm Cara."

"I am." He shook her hand surprised at her grip strength. Jordan had said she was ex-military, but if her physique was any indication, she still worked out as if she were active. "Did Tia get settled all right?"

"I suppose. I haven't checked on her since I showed her to her room, but you're welcome to now. She's in room three down that hallway." Cara turned and pointed behind her. "I've got a dinner to prepare for."

"Thank you." Brody headed the direction she had pointed and paused when he reached room three. He felt like a high schooler again, showing up for a first date. It was an odd feeling considering he was over thirty years old, but it didn't change the fact that his heart thundered loudly in his chest and his palms had collected a wet sheen. He ran them down his pants leg and then curled his right hand into a fist to knock.

"Come on in. It's open," came Tia's voice from inside the room. He pushed the door open to find her sitting on the bed. "I didn't have much to unpack and nothing else to do," she said with a shrug as if answering his unspoken question. "Cara said I could watch TV in the living room, but I didn't feel like it. Do you think while we're out, we can stop by an electronics store so I can get a new phone and computer?"

A grin tugged at Brody's lips. "We can stop wherever you would like. I figured we could get dinner and then possibly hit a clothing store, but we can add an electronics store in as well."

She pushed herself off the bed and grabbed her crutches. "You would go to a clothing store with me?"

"Yes?" he asked hesitantly, not knowing if this was a trick question or not. He hadn't gone to many clothing stores with Rachel but only because he never really thought about it.

She laughed at him. "It's just that most men don't like waiting around for women to try on clothes."

Ah, now that made sense. He supposed that would get boring if she spent too long there, but he also knew she had spent the last week in a hospital gown and had nothing except what Jordan had brought her. He would wait all night if it meant she was able to find some clothes to make her feel more comfortable. "Well, I think you'll find I'm not most men."

She had reached his side by the time he spoke, and she turned her blue eyes up at him. A slight smile sent the corners of her mouth twitching in an adorable manner, but her voice was low and sultry when she spoke. "I think I've already realized that."

He felt the pull between them, the desire to kiss her, but it was too soon. He hadn't kissed a woman since Rachel, and he wanted to do it right. So, instead he cleared his throat and motioned to the door. "Shall we go?"

Confusion flashed in her eyes for a moment, but then she put on a smile and nodded. He followed her out mentally berating himself for confusing her. She'd been through enough bad experiences to last a lifetime; she didn't need him adding to her confusion.

When they reached the car, he held the door open for her and helped her in before loading her crutches in the back. As he walked to his side, the hairs on the back of his neck rose. He felt as if someone was watching them. With a surreptitious glance, he scanned the area, but he saw no one. Perhaps it was just a nosy neighbor watching out a window. He would scan the windows as they drove off. No need worrying Tia if it was nothing. He drove past the other houses slowly glad for the low speed limit, but there was no one in any of the windows. Probably just his overactive imagination then.

Though he rarely went out anymore, Brody had scheduled a dinner at an upscale Italian restaurant. "I hope you don't mind Italian," he said as he pulled the car into a space. "I suppose I should have asked."

She flashed him a wide grin. "I love

Italian. In fact, I love cheese and bread and pasta of all kinds which is why I do yoga."

"Well good," he said with a chuckle, "we are in the right place then."

CHAPTER 16

Tia followed Brody out of the restaurant feeling a little like Cinderella, underdressed and out of her element. Though she'd enjoyed dinner immensely, she'd felt people's eyes on them. The rest of the diners wore button down shirts and dresses while she was in the pants Jordan had brought her. She couldn't wait to get to the clothing store and pick up some new clothes for occasions like these. Assuming there were more occasions.

When Brody had picked her up from Cara's, there had been a moment. A moment where she thought he was going to kiss her, where she wanted him to kiss her, but then he hadn't. She knew it probably had more to do with the loss of his wife, but it had still sent the insecurity fluttering in her stomach. What if he decided she wasn't interesting enough now that she was out of the hospital? What if what he thought was attraction was more what they called 'Rescue Romance' and now that she didn't need to be saved, the attraction had faded?

"Did you get enough to eat?" Brody asked as they stepped into the cool evening air. The sun hadn't set completely, but the last orange, pink, and red rays were low on the horizon.

"I did," Tia said with a laugh. "It's probably a good thing I'm wearing stretchy pants or I might have popped a button, but I promise I'll dress nicer next time."

"I think you look beautiful," Brody said as he opened the car door.

Their gazes locked again, and Tia felt the pull once more. His eyes peered into her soul, and she opened every door to him, willing him to kiss her. A light breeze traipsed across her arms sending goosebumps erupting on her skin. Her breath stilled as her lips parted and his face lowered to hers. When his lips touched hers, sparks darted through her body and though it was crazy, she felt as if she were experiencing her last 'first kiss.' Even more, she felt the last of the locks on her memory fall away. She gasped and pulled away from him.

"What? Was it awful?" he asked. "I know I'm out of practice."

She placed a finger against his lips to stop his ramblings and smiled. "I remember, Brody. Everything."

Light radiated from his face as he threw his arms around her. "That's wonderful." And then he kissed her again, slow and deliberately. Her body trembled with emotion. "So, do we still head to a store or do we head to your place?" he asked when he pulled back.

Her face fell and the joyful emotions she had just experienced vanished. "I didn't have a place here. I'd expected the meeting with Rico to go quickly. I thought I could use my good looks to persuade him." She dropped her eyes to the ground, embarrassed by her choices. "Oh gosh, I was an awful person."

"Hey," he said putting a finger under her chin and tilting it up. "You might not have made the best decisions in your past, but we are all guilty of that. You have a Savior who forgives you, and you have the opportunity to make new choices from here on out."

"Do you think it's really that easy? Can I

just forget my past?" She wanted him to say yes, but that old insecurity that had driven her to do horrible things whispered that he wouldn't want her now that he knew what she was really like. How could anyone want her?

He brushed her hair behind her ear, his fingertips lighting up the nerves in her face. "No, you may never forget it, but you can apologize for what you need to and learn from the rest. Your past doesn't have to define your future."

"Hmm, that is sound advice," she said breathlessly. Did he realize his words could also apply to him though in a slightly different way? He'd lost someone he loved, but he didn't have to let that be the end of his story either.

"Yeah, I guess it is." His eyes stared into hers again before closing as he leaned down. Before his lips touched hers, the sound of an engine revving grabbed Tia's attention.

She turned her head to see a vehicle heading their direction. It was going fast, too fast, and the night of the accident came flooding back. Her body froze as she saw the headlights in her mirror again, blinding her.

"Tia? You okay?" Brody's voice seemed

far away as she watched the vehicle come toward them, helpless to do anything. "Tia."

The vehicle roared past them, and Tia blinked. "I'm sorry," she said. "That car - I heard the engine rev - and the lights reminded me of the accident. I couldn't move."

"Hey, it's okay," he said running his hands down her arms. "You're going to be okay. It's going to take some time to heal completely. How about we hit that department store and then I take you home? I think you could use some rest."

"Yeah, thanks." Tia's head was still spinning and her heart was still pounding though as she buckled her seatbelt. She'd been so sure that vehicle was out to get them. Would she ever relax again?

BRODY SIGHED as he walked back to his car after dropping Tia off at Cara's place. She'd been so relaxed at dinner and then the car revving its engine had sent her back into her shell. Even the trip to the department store and an hour of trying on clothing hadn't brought her back entirely. He wondered if she would always be chasing shadows.

As he unlocked the car, a movement out of the corner of his eye caught his attention. He turned to see what it was, but only darkness stared back at him. Probably a raccoon or some other night animal out scrounging for garbage. Here he was worried about Tia relaxing and he couldn't even calm himself down. He thought he'd seen something when he picked her up and now again when he dropped her off. Perhaps he needed a good night's sleep as well. He certainly had been on edge all week. In fact, he didn't think he'd had a decent night's sleep since Tia's car accident. He would remedy that tonight.

As he turned back around, he got only a glimpse of the man before pain shot through his head and the world went dark.

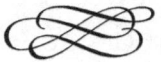

CHAPTER 17

"How was your date?" Cara asked as Tia sat down in one of the chairs in the living room. She hadn't meant to disturb Cara's reading, but she also didn't feel like going to her room alone yet.

"It was…." she hesitated as she set her crutches on the floor beside her, "good."

"That's not very convincing," Cara said sticking a bookmark in her book and shutting the cover to get Tia her full attention. "What happened?"

Tia sighed. She wished she had a better answer for that question. "Brody is great. He opened the doors for me, and we had a wonderful dinner at a little Italian place. Then he kissed me, and the rest of my memory came back."

Cara tilted her head and tiny wrinkles appeared on her forehead as she furrowed her brow. "That all sounds better than good - I mean the man kissed you. And that was good right?"

Heat crept up Tia's face. "Yeah, that part was perfect. No complaints for sure."

Cara grinned and pulled her feet up under her. "So, I'm guessing there's more to it."

Tia nodded. "There's two more pieces. The first one is my past. I was not a nice person, and I think I went down that road because of my father, but still... How do I date this amazing man who is practically a saint while I have this checkered past?" Her gaze dropped to her hands and she picked at a rogue cuticle. "I mean I'm only here because I flew out to try and convince a man to promote my book. And I was willing to use almost any means necessary."

Cara's head bobbed as she let out a long breath. "Yeah, I can see why you feel that way. Does Brody know?"

"A little," Tia said with a shrug. "I haven't

told him everything yet. I'm afraid he'll run away."

"He might." Cara's matter-of-fact tone caused Tia to raise her head. "But if he does, then he's not the man for you."

Tia's mouth fell open. That was certainly not the advice she had been looking for.

"Look, that's a hard lesson for a woman to learn at any point. I haven't dated a lot, but I gave my heart to this guy once who said all the right things until it came time for the rubber to meet the road. Then he was nowhere to be found - wouldn't return my texts or calls. I spent a few days wondering what I had done wrong, analyzing the relationship, agonizing over it really. But then I realized, it wasn't me. It was him. He wasn't ready for a real relationship with me. If Brody runs from your past, then it's just a sign you aren't meant to be together, and it would be better to find out now than to date for months and find out then."

"I suppose you're right." Tia wished she had Cara's confidence, but growing up feeling unloved by her father had fertilized this insecurity in her that she wasn't good enough until it had taken root and overrun her life.

"You said there were two reasons. What is

the second one that is keeping you from smiling and walking on cloud nine?"

Tia dropped her eyes back to her fingers. She pulled off the rogue cuticle, grimacing slightly at the pain that shot through her finger momentarily. "When we left the restaurant, I heard this car rev its engine and I thought it was coming right toward us. I froze and couldn't move until the car passed us. It reminded me so much of the accident, and I thought someone out there was still after me." She lifted her eyes. "I don't know how to stop being afraid."

Sympathy and understanding flooded Cara's eyes and she leaned forward. "That will come with time too. You've been through a traumatic experience. You can't expect it's going to be unicorns and rainbows right away. I still have nightmares about my deployments sometimes. I'll see bombs exploding or injured civilians in my dreams." She chuffed out a breath and ran her hand through her spiky hair. "And don't get me started on loud noises. I still jump. Fourth of July is no longer my favorite holiday, but it gets easier. Every day will get a little…"

Her words stopped abruptly as the lights in the house went out and darkness filled the room. The mood in the room shifted and Tia could feel the fear pressing against her. She didn't believe this was a simple case of the electricity going out. There had been no storm, no reason. No reason except her.

"Tia, do you have Jordan's number on you?" Cara asked in a forceful whisper.

"I do, but I don't have a phone." Why had they forgotten to stop at the electronics store on the way home? "And I don't know this place well enough to go stumbling around in the dark." There was no way she could navigate her own home in the dark on crutches. She certainly couldn't do it in this house she didn't know.

"I'm going to hand you my cell phone. There's a hall closet about fifteen feet to your left and nothing is blocking your way. I want you to crawl that direction as quietly and quickly as possible. Get inside, shut the door, and call Jordan."

"What are you going to do?" Tia's voice trembled with the fear racing through her.

"I'm going to do what I said I'd do. I'm going to protect you. Now go."

Tia didn't need a second urging. As soon as she felt the phone hit her palm, she lowered herself to the floor and began crawling the direction Tia had said. Her cast made a soft scratching sound as it dragged across the floor, and her breath sounded like a freight train in her head. Surely, she was giving her location away as silence filled the rest of the house.

When she had gone approximately fifteen feet, she began to feel around for the door of the closet. With every second her hand didn't find it, her anxiety increased until she nearly screamed for joy when her fingers finally found the knob.

She opened the door and crawled inside, shutting it after her. Only then did she turn on Cara's cell phone, grab the card Jordan had given her from her pocket, and dial the number.

"Jordan?" she asked in a hoarse whisper when he picked up.

"Tia? What's wrong?"

"I'm at Cara's, but someone's here. The electricity just went off. Cara sent me to the closet to call you." Just then the door swung open and the light from a flashlight blinded her.

"Hello, Tia, I've been looking for you."

At the sound of the man's voice, Tia screamed and dropped the phone.

"Tia? Tia?"

❦

THE SOUND of a scream stirred Brody. He struggled to open his eyes, but the pain in his head was severe. He reached a hand up and was not surprised to find it come away sticky with blood. What had the man hit him with? More importantly, was Tia okay?

Another scream carried out of the house. Groaning with effort, he pushed himself up. He wanted to rush into the house, but the spinning of the world around him forced him to wait. Rushing in without all his faculties wouldn't help anyone. He pulled his phone out and dialed 911 while the world slowed down.

"911, what's your emergency?"

"My name is Dr. Brody Cavanaugh. I'm at 212 Whistler Avenue. I've been attacked and I think the attacker is in the house with hostages."

"I'm sending help. Please stay on the line until they arrive."

Brody knew that's what he should do. He was certainly in no shape to help Tia much, but he couldn't sit out here and do nothing. He couldn't let another woman he cared for die. "I'm sorry; I have to see if I can help," he said before ending the call.

He pocketed the phone and then stood testing his vision and balance. Another deep breath and he felt okay to move. The only problem was he had no weapon. Nothing but his hands and with the blow to the head, he didn't trust their power or their efficiency.

He scanned the area for anything he could use, and then he remembered the tire iron in his car. Popping the trunk, he grabbed it and headed for the house. Brody had never wielded a weapon at anyone, but if it meant saving Tia's life, he would.

The dark house was silent as he approached. Fear that he was too late raced through his body as he pushed open the door. He wished he had a flashlight as he didn't know the layout of Cara's house, but with the front door open, a little light spilled in from the outside. Enough for him to see a few feet in front of him. The immediate area was deserted. He had two choices; he could turn left toward the bedrooms or right toward the kitchen and living room area.

A scuffling sound to his right sent him that direction and a moment later, the soft light of a flashlight illuminated the room. Tia sat on a chair tears streaming down her face as she stared into the barrel of a gun.

"Don't come any farther or I'll shoot," the man said as if sensing Brody's approach. As he glanced Brody's direction, Brody saw Cara out of the corner of his eye. She was trying to get the jump on the man, but she couldn't get in the right position unless the man was facing Brody.

"Who are you and what do you want with Tia?"

The man smiled and turned his attention back to Tia. Cara ducked down in just the nick of time. "Why don't you ask Tia that?"

Brody looked to Tia trying desperately to come up with a plan to get the man focused on him.

"This is Rico," Tia said, her voice cracking with emotion. "It was you on the patio and in the doorway, wasn't it? I thought it was the other man, Adrian, but it was you."

Rico nodded and waved his hands out for a minute as if bowing. "So, it was. You could have left – should have left when I told you and all of this could have been avoided, but you didn't. You had to come back and become a loose end."

"But I didn't hear anything," Tia said. "I had no idea what you were discussing."

"Maybe not, but you were seen leaving and you left evidence. I couldn't let you live after that. It would have jeopardized my authority."

Realization dawned on Brody. "You're the head of the drug ring, aren't you? Not Adrian."

Rico's head shot his direction. "Adrian was too rash to be head of the organization. He planned better than my wife, but he still got caught. Him and his wife. Besides, he was known. I managed to keep my cover in place and lead a profitable life here in Fire Beach on the side."

"Except they know about you now," Brody said hoping to keep Rico's attention on him long enough for Cara to strike. "The police know all about your connections in Chicago. Your publishing company will fold, your wife is going to jail, and the Chicago police won't rest until they destroy your organization."

"The only one who will be destroyed tonight is you….." Cara was in position and Brody held his breath hoping Rico wouldn't turn her direction. "And her." His gun swung back toward Tia, and his face was just a moment behind, but it was long enough for Cara to spring up and ram her head directly into Rico's chest. The gun went flying as he crashed to the floor, and the sound of the gunshot filled the air leaving a ringing in Brody's ears.

He glanced first toward Tia, but though shaken, she appeared uninjured, so he turned his attention to Cara who lay on the floor, her arms wrapped tightly around Rico's neck, and her muscular legs pinning his arms to his body even though he writhed against her.

"What do you have to secure him with?" Brody asked looking around the room.

"Zip ties," Cara grunted. "Over in the desk drawer."

Brody followed the motion of her head and could just make out the form of a desk. He hurried over and rifled through the drawers until he found the zip ties. Grabbing them, he returned to Cara and secured the man's hands together. Only then did she let up her grip on him.

"Thanks," she said shaking out her arms. "He's a strong one."

Rico said nothing as he watched them

with his icy stare. "How did you manage to secure him so quickly?" Brody asked.

She ran a hand down her thighs as if to loosen those muscles as well. "MMA training in college. It wasn't as big for women back then, so I used to wrestle with all the guys. There's a reason they called me Leech. Once I grab on, I don't let go."

Somehow Brody didn't doubt that. "Good work," he said before turning to Tia. "Are you okay?"

"Shaken up, but okay," she said but her eyes stay focused on the man on the floor. "Will this ever stop?"

"Hey." He placed his hands on either side of her face and tilted it up until she was looking at him. "We'll figure this out. Together."

Her eyes widened when she saw his head. "You're hurt!"

"Yeah, I'll need to get checked out, but I'll be okay too."

A moment later, Jordan, Al, and two other men Brody vaguely recognized filed into the room. The two men grabbed Rico while Al attended to Tia and Jordan sauntered over to Cara.

"Thank you. I knew you were the right woman for the job."

She shot him a glare as she massaged her forearms. "Next time, a little warning of what I might be facing would be nice."

"I would have warned you except we didn't know what to expect. We thought it was over after the attempt at the hospital, but we didn't realize Rico was not just the front for the organization - he was the head."

"Yeah, we know," Cara said, "He had a hard time keeping his mouth shut."

"Does that mean it's really over now?" Tia asked.

"It does. Rico's going away for a long time along with his wife and the Petrovs. You may have to testify, but we all owe you a debt of gratitude. I know it wasn't your intent, but through your actions, you've managed to help us take down a pretty large drug organization."

Brody smiled and squeezed Tia's shoulder. "See? I told you everything happens for a reason. I think you've just made up for a lot of the mistakes in your past."

"Thank you," she said and when she smiled up at him, Brody knew she was going to be okay.

CHAPTER 18

ia woke more rested the next morning than she had in a long time. Some of it was probably not sleeping in a hospital room, but she knew some of it was finally feeling as if she were home and safe. Even in her old life, she'd had no friends like Brody, Cara, and Jordan - people willing to risk their lives to keep her safe. It was nice. And humbling. And today Brody was going to take her to lunch before she started her first shift at Fire Dreams.

She couldn't remember the last time she had worked in a restaurant, but she was looking forward to it today. Actually, she was just looking forward to not being in a hospital, being shot at, poisoned, or run over. It had been a long week, and one she would probably never forget.

Pushing back the covers, she rolled out of bed and hobbled over to the bag of clothes she had bought the night before. She hadn't even managed to unpack with all the craziness of Rico, and she definitely wanted to take a bath before she fully dressed. That was another thing she hadn't done properly in the last week. She'd have preferred a shower but supposed it was out of the question. Surely, she wouldn't have to only do baths until the cast came off though. She'd have to ask Brody when she saw him for lunch.

After grabbing clothes to change into, Tia grabbed her crutches and made her way the few feet to the bathroom. The bath proved to be challenging since she couldn't get her cast wet, but after a few tries, she managed to get her foot positioned in just the right way that it was out of the water while most of the rest of her was in. Though she normally didn't like baths, this one held just the right remedy to wash her fears and anxiety away.

When she was dry and dressed - another adventure she would not miss when this cast came off, she crutched down the hall to the dining area. Cara had a display of food laid out - eggs, waffles, fruit, coffee, juice.

"Good morning, Tia. How did you sleep?" Cara asked as she placed a large plate of pancakes down as well.

"Actually, pretty well. How long have you been up cooking this breakfast?"

Cara laughed. "I know, it's overkill, but I cooked a lot in my unit. Got used to feeding a dozen hungry soldiers. Guess old habits die hard, but don't worry the guy in room one will eat half of this when he gets up."

Tia shook her head as she imagined the stomachache she would have if she ate even half of this. "I'll just get some eggs and fruit."

"You sit," Cara said pointing to a chair, "and I'll get what you want and bring it to you. Jordan and Brody would have my hide if you tripped trying to carry food and injured yourself at my house."

Tia laughed but she could see it. "Okay, okay. Eggs, oranges, and coffee please. With cream if you have it."

"Of course I have it." Cara loaded up a plate and set it before Tia before filling a cup and returning with it and the creamer carafe. "So, what's on your agenda for today?" she asked as she grabbed her own coffee mug and sat across from Tia.

"Brody is coming by in an hour or so. I think he planned an early movie and then lunch before my shift at Fire Dreams." She smiled as she speared a little egg and shoveled it in her mouth. Her day sounded so ordinary - a welcome sound after the last week.

"He roped you into working for him, did he?" Cara picked up her cup and took a sip.

"He did, but only until I get back on my feet. Now that I remember everything, I want to get back to writing soon, but I need to do a few things first. Make some apologies, buy a new computer, move my stuff here."

Cara raised a brow as she leaned back in her chair. "You plan to stay then?"

Tia grinned as she peeled the orange. "I do. I think there's definitely some things worth staying here for."

"Good. I'm glad to hear it. This town could use a little excitement."

Tia laughed so hard she nearly spat her food out. "You don't think the last week counted as excitement?"

"Nah," Cara said with a flick of her wrist. "That's not what I mean. We need some excitement people can get behind, and I think a romance author writing about our town might be just the ticket. Be good for business."

"Well, I'll do what I can," Tia said with a smile.

❦

BRODY SMILED as he spied Tia behind the counter. She not only looked lighter without the weight of fear on her shoulders, but she looked at home greeting guests as they entered the restaurant.

"Brody." Her mouth broke into a wide grin when she spied him. "Let me clock out and I'll be ready to go."

"Take your time," he said as he watched her crutch off to the back room.

"She's kind of a natural," Jordan said coming up beside him. "I hope she decides to stick around a while."

Brody smiled at the man he now considered a friend. "She is. Told me this morning when I picked her up. She wants to go to California and make amends and get her affairs in order, but then she plans to find a place to rent locally."

"Glad to hear it. She seems like a completely different person here."

Brody shook his head. "No, she seems like the sweet woman I believe she was until greed corrupted her. I just hope she stays that way."

Jordan put a hand on his shoulder. "With a good man like you by her side, I can't see her taking that path again."

"Are you two talking about me?" Tia asked with a smile as she approached them.

"Just telling Brody what a good job you're doing," Jordan said.

"Good, then I hope you won't mind if I ask for a week off? I want to close the chapter on my life in California, so I can start fresh here."

"I think that's a great idea, and I'm fairly certain I can convince the owner to give you a week even though you just started." He gave her a friendly smile before excusing himself to take care of a customer.

"Will you come with me?" she asked Brody as he held the restaurant door open. "To California? I don't think I can do it alone."

Brody wanted to say yes, but a trip with her? That was a big step. And it would require more time off work. However, he hadn't taken a day since Rachel died. He had enough days saved up, and he hadn't taken a vacation in years. Besides, if he really wanted Tia to make a change, then he needed to support her in any way possible. If that meant a trip to California, then he guessed he could take a little more time off. "I'll be with you every step of the way."

She leaned up and placed a kiss on his lips. "I don't deserve you Brody Cavanaugh, but I'm going to thank God every day for sending you into my life."

Brody returned her smile and thought he might do exactly the same thing.

CHAPTER 19

ia stood outside the door of Ava's office and took a deep breath. She wanted to apologize, but actually being here was another thing entirely. What if Ava slammed the door in her face? What if Justin kicked her out? They had both agreed to meet her here when Tia called, but what if it was just to tease her about how far she'd fallen?

"You have to knock," Brody said beside her.

She looked up at him, a pained smile on her face. "I know, but what if they slam the door in my face? I was so awful to them."

He laced his fingers through hers and squeezed. "They won't. Besides, you aren't the same person anymore."

Right. She wasn't the same person anymore. She no longer cared solely for money. Not after four attempts on her life. Her priorities had definitely shifted, and while she did want to make enough money to take care of herself and her mother as she'd promised herself so long ago, she no longer needed to be the best. Just being Tia seemed like enough.

She raised her hand and knocked on the door. A moment later, it swung open and Ava McDermott stared back at her. "Hello, Tia," she said with a slight smile. She stepped back and held the door open. "Won't you come in?"

Tia squeezed Brody's hand one more time before letting go of it to crutch into the waiting area of Ava's office. Justin sat in one of the chairs there and rose as they approached. For a moment, no one said anything and the silence sat heavy in the room.

Tia cleared her throat, forcing her nerves to stop fluttering. "Thank you for agreeing to see me."

"You said it was important," Ava said as she sat down and motioned for everyone else to do the same.

"It is." Tia glanced over at Brody who smiled and motioned for her to continue. "I came to apologize to you. To you both. A few weeks ago, I landed in the wrong place at the wrong time, and it almost killed me, but as I healed, I realized how awful I'd been. I'm working to change, but before I could, I needed to apologize to those I've wronged." She chuckled ruefully. "It's been an awfully long list."

Justin glanced over at Ava and then back at Tia. "We're sorry for whatever you've been through, Tia. It appears like a lot, but we forgave you a long time ago."

Tia's eyes widened and she blinked at them. "You did?"

"Of course we did," Ava said. "None of us are perfect, and we both know that we've made poor decisions in our past as well, but God has forgiven us. However, we couldn't gain that forgiveness from Him if we didn't also forgive those who wronged us."

Tears filled Tia's eyes, blinding her vision for a moment. "You two are both so amazing. I hope that I can learn from your compassion."

Ava smiled at her. "I think you already have."

BRODY STARED at the woman next to him as they drove to their final destination before returning home. Though her fingers still sported acrylic nails, nothing else about her appearance looked like the rich woman he had first seen when he pulled her from the wrecked sports car.

Her long blonde hair was pulled back in a simple loose pony, and her outfit was a simple t-shirt and shorts with no designer tag in sight. He'd wondered if she might revert when she saw her old things and outfits in her apartment, but instead she'd decided to hire someone to sell it all and send her the money. "That way I don't have to pay to have it shipped," she'd said, but he thought it was because those things no longer suited her.

She still was very different from Rachel, more extroverted than she'd been and able to spit words out faster than he could listen half the time, especially when she was excited, but despite her differences, she had one vital thing in common – the ability to make him feel like he was the only man in the room and that he could do anything. He'd certainly proved that to himself over the last few weeks as his healing hand and head proved.

"You ready?" he asked as he pulled up in front of the run-down trailer. He had a hard time believing that this was where she had grown up, but recognition mingled with fear covered her face, and he knew it was true.

Her shoulders pulled back with her breath. "Yeah, I guess I am," but her eyes stared out the window and he wondered if she really were. It was one thing to apologize to people you once considered friends. It was another thing entirely to apologize to the woman you promised to provide for her and then failed.

Brody turned off the ignition and walked around to Tia's side to help her out. He handed her the crutches from the back seat and followed her up the overgrown pathway to the front door. She paused, took another deep breath, and then knocked on the door.

A moment later, the door swung open and a woman who looked like a much older version of Tia opened the door. Her blonde hair was streaked with gray and from the wrinkles and age spots dotting her face, it appeared life had not been easy on her. Beside him, Tia sniffed and covered her mouth with her hand.

But the woman's face transformed as recognition dawned in her eyes, and a smile lit her face. "Tia?"

"Hi, Momma. I know I'm a little late, but I came to fulfill my promise."

Tears filled the woman's eyes and she pulled Tia in for a hug. "I never gave up hope, Tia. Even when you stopped calling and coming by, I prayed God would send you home one day, and He has." She pulled back holding Tia by the upper arms, and then her eyes flicked to the side. "And you've brought a friend. Who is this?"

"Dr. Brody Cavanaugh, ma'am. It's a pleasure to meet you." He held out his hand and the woman smiled as she shook it.

"A doctor? Well, I have missed a lot. How about you come inside and we can catch up?" She stepped back and held the door open, and Brody followed Tia into the home she had grown up in.

The inside, though sparse, was neat and tidy. Her mother led them to the living room and a well-worn couch where they sat and stared at one another for an uncomfortable moment. "Can I get you something to drink?" the woman asked.

"No Momma, we aren't staying long."

The woman's face fell. "Oh, well, I'm glad you stopped by for as long as you could."

"Momma, I want you to come back to Fire Beach with me."

The woman blinked at her. "I don't... what do you mean?"

Tia leaned forward and took her mother's hands. "I've missed too much the last few years, Mom. I don't want to miss any more time with you. I've sold my home in California and I'm moving to Fire Beach to start over. I'd like you to come with me."

"But...but I have a job here."

"And you can have one there if you want. I know a great restaurant that's going to need a hostess when I return to writing, but you've worked your entire life for me, so I could have a better life. Now, I'd like to give back to you. I've already found the perfect place. All it's missing is you."

Brody held his breath as he watched emotions flutter across Tia's mother's face. If she said no, Tia would be crushed, but she had prepared herself for the possibility as they drove here. However, he hoped she said yes.

Family was important, and he knew being able to provide for her mother would be the final block in Tia's healing process.

"What do I need to bring?" her mother finally said as she smiled widely at Tia.

"Nothing, Momma, just you." Forgetting her crutches, Tia launched herself out of the couch and into her mother's arms. Brody smiled at the touching scene. Somehow, he felt that no matter what life threw at her now, Tia would be all right.

THE EPILOGUE

Two Months Later

TIA SMILED at the group of people around the table. She'd met so many wonderful friends over the last few weeks. Cassidy, Jordan's girlfriend, had quickly become one of her closest friends along with Cara, and because of that she'd met many of the other firemen sitting around the table – Bubba, Luca, Deacon, and Ivy, the paramedic.

There was also her mother, Brody and his friend Nick, Jordan's brother Graham, and some of the other police officers on Jordan's unit. She'd never had such a great group of friends in her life, and she couldn't believe they had all wanted to celebrate her book release. She had decided not to pursue another publisher but to self-publish this book because she hadn't wanted a company to demand changes. This was her story, and it needed to be told exactly the way she had written it.

"Thank you all for coming," Jordan said as he banged his water glass with a spoon to quiet the chatter. "As you all know, we have a resident celebrity in our midst."

Tia ducked her eyes as heat flared up her cheeks. This was way too much.

"And she has finally finished her masterpiece. Tia get up here and show off your beautiful book."

Tia shook her head as she pushed back her chair. She loved that they cared enough about her to want to celebrate her accomplishment, but she would have been just as happy to do a small get together instead of this large party Jordan had thrown for her. However, he was still her boss, and it appeared to make him happy, so she had agreed.

She grabbed the bag which held her book and walked to the front of the table. Her cast was gone and her injuries had healed except for the scar that still ran across her forehead, but Tia didn't mind. She now considered it a badge of honor – her second chance at life.

"Thank you all for wanting to celebrate this with me. This wasn't an easy book to write, but your support helped me get past all the hard parts, and while I've loved a lot of books I've written, I think this might be my best."

"Hear hear," Brody said lifting his glass and flashing her a large smile. "What?" he asked as he looked around the table. "I already read it, so I know that it's good."

She shook her head and smiled at him. "Anyway, I think it is because of all of you that it turned out so well, and that's why I'm pleased to present to you..." she paused for dramatic effect as she pulled the book out of the bag, "The Key to Remember."

Cheers and clapping sounded as Tia passed the book around the table.

"Hey, this might even be a book you could read, Luca," Bubba teased as he flipped through the pages.

"Only if it's on audiobook," Luca shot back. "I can't sit still long enough to read a paper book. Sorry, Tia."

She laughed and shook her head as the teasing comments continued to flow around the table. Brody caught her eye and flashed her a wink, and Tia didn't think she'd ever felt more loved than she did right now.

"Excuse me?"

The conversation stilled at the unfamiliar voice, and they all turned to see a petite woman in the doorway.

"I'm sorry to interrupt, but do any of you know where I can find Matt Parker?"

Confused glances shot around the room and Jordan stood to address her. "I'm sorry, ma'am, there's no Matt Parker here."

"Actually, there is."

Time seemed to freeze as every eye turned to Bubba as he pushed back his chair and stood. "I'm Matt Parker."

If you want to know what Bubba's story is, be sure to order your copy of *Never Forget the Past* today!

PART I
WHEN QUESTIONS ABOUND

Here is a special sneak peek at the companion short story, "When Questions Abound." Remember you can get this for free if you send me a copy of your receipt or the first word of chapter 10 to loranahoopes@gmail.com

CHAPTER 1

"Help! Is there a doctor in here?"

Detective Jordan Graves pulled his attention from his girlfriend Cassidy to see who needed assistance. A man stood in the doorway of the restaurant, a frantic look on his face. "There was an accident. A woman's been injured, but the guy who hit her took off. She looks bad though. Are any of you doctors?"

"I am." Dr. Brody Cavanaugh fought his way through the crowd followed by two or three other people Jordan recognized from the hospital.

"We better go too," Jordan said to Cassidy. He flashed an apologetic look at Graham, his brother and co-owner of Fire Dreams before hurrying outside with the rest of the crowd. The sun had set, but the streetlights illuminated the area and down the street Jordan could see the car – a red sports car – folded in a "C" shape.

"Get the Jaws of Life," Bubba, one of the firemen, ordered as he sprinted towards the car. Around him, the rest of the firemen spread out. Some ran toward the firehouse a block away to get the truck and ambulance, and others followed Bubba including Cassidy.

Jordan glanced around for the man who had entered the restaurant. He stood a few feet away wringing his hands together. "You." Jordan hurried over to the man. "I'm Detective Graves. Did you see the accident happen?" He pulled out his notepad to write down the details.

"It happened so fast. I heard the crash and then it sounded like he gunned it. Why would he gun it if he knew he'd hurt someone?" The man was rambling, clearly in shock.

"Can you tell me what the vehicle looked like that hit her?" The man turned to face Jordan and for a moment his eyes were clear. "It was a truck. A black Ford truck."

"Did you see anything else? A license number by chance?" Jordan asked.

"It just drove off. Why would anyone do that?" Clearly this man wasn't going to be of any more help. His state of shock was simply too great. At least for now.

"Can I get your name?" Jordan asked. Perhaps the man would remember more when the shock wore off.

"It's Ethan. Ethan Bower."

Jordan took down the name and number of the man though he doubted they would contact him again. He appeared to have supplied as much as he could.

Having finished his interview of the witness, Jordan walked over to the wrecked car. The firemen had succeeded in getting the woman out and the ambulance had driven off a few minutes ago. That left the car as his domain. His and Al's, his female partner.

"Find anything yet?"

Al was already poking around inside the car. She popped her head out and held up a mangled phone. "Found this, but there's no purse, no wallet. I haven't checked the trunk yet, but I can't find anything to let us know who this woman was. Did you get anything from the witness?"

"Not much. He said he heard the wreck while he was closing shop. When he looked, the black truck was speeding off. He didn't get a license plate number."

Al sighed and crossed her arms. "We better hope the driver makes it then because all I have right now is a lot of questions."

Jordan agreed. "Can you pop the trunk?"

Al leaned back inside but though he could see her tugging on the lever, nothing was happening. "Is it working?"

"No, it must have gotten damaged in the accident." He scanned the area. Bubba and Luca were just putting the Jaws of Life back on the truck. "Bubba, can you guys use that on the trunk? We can't get it to open."

"Wish you'd said something earlier," Bubba said with a teasing smile. "This thing isn't exactly light, but Luca could use the extra workout."

"Speak for yourself," Luca retorted.

Jordan stepped back as the two large men approached. The hum of machinery filled the air again until they were able to cut a hole allowing access to the trunk. Jordan joined Al at the back as Bubba and Luca headed back to the truck. With her flashlight, they examined the trunk, but there was nothing there either.

"Guess that's it," Al said.

"Yeah, I'll write down the license plate number and we can run it tomorrow. Perhaps that will give us something to go on."

"Sounds good. Sorry the opening of your restaurant was interrupted, but it looks like it will be a great place."

Jordan looked back at the restaurant he and Graham had worked so hard to open. It certainly wasn't the opening night they had planned for, but he hoped this night wouldn't keep people from coming back. "Thanks, Al. I hope so. Guess I'll see you tomorrow."

CHAPTER 2

"Sir, I'd like permission to investigate this hit and run further," Jordan said as he looked at his notes from the night before.

"You have reason to believe it was more than an accident?" Jack Stone, head of the unit, asked as he looked at the board of their current cases. It was rather quiet at the moment for which Jordan was glad.

"Just a feeling sir. The witness said the truck didn't even bother to slow down which was supported by the lack of brake marks at the scene. Plus, we found no wallet, no purse, nothing in the car besides the woman's cell phone. It just feels wrong." Jordan had no concrete evidence that it was anything but an accident, but he had long ago learned to trust his gut. And his gut was telling him there was more to this case.

Stone turned from the board and fixed Jordan with his classic stony stare. "Two days. If something hasn't come up that proves this wasn't an accident, you let it go. Understood?"

"Crystal. Thank you, sir." He looked over at Al who was working on something at her desk. "Al, you want to come with me to the hospital? I'd like to see if our victim made it and if she remembers anything."

Al nodded and grabbed the mangled phone. "Yep, let's go. I was looking for traffic cams, but there was nothing pointed at that intersection."

Figured. Even with all the traffic cameras in the city, they rarely seemed to catch a break from them on any case they worked. "Hopefully, our victim will have some information."

A few minutes later, they pulled into the hospital parking lot. After a brief stop at the desk to sign in and declare their weapons, they headed toward the ICU.

"I was hoping we would find you here," Jordan said as he spied Dr. Brody Cavanaugh near the main ICU desk studying a clipboard. "Brody, this is my partner, Al Parker. The woman had a phone in the car," he said holding up the object, "but no wallet. Is she awake yet?"

Brody glanced up at them. "She is, but she doesn't remember anything. Not even her name."

Al blinked at him. "Is that normal? Will she get it back?"

Brody shrugged as he replaced one clipboard and picked up another. "I don't know. She hit her head pretty hard and sustained a concussion, but the CT didn't show any lasting damage although it did show swelling. My guess is that she will, but I can't give you a timeline."

Memory loss was certainly not what Jordan had been hoping for, but perhaps with the right questions they could jog her memory. "Is she able to talk? Can we ask her some questions?"

Brody regarded Jordan and flashed a concerned stare. "She is capable of speaking but don't push her too hard. Rest is important for her right now, and again, I don't think she remembers much. Although she does think someone was after her."

Jordan's ears perked up at that. "She does? What did she say?"

"Not much," Brody said with a shrug. "Just that she remembered being afraid and thought someone was after her. I was about to refer her to psych for an examination."

Jordan's jaw clenched, and he exchanged a glance with Al. "Hold off on that for a while, will you? She might be right. We found no brake marks on the road and our witness said the truck didn't even try to stop. My gut says this might not have been an accident, and we are determined to find out who hit her and why. Which room is she in?"

"Room six." Brody pointed behind him.

Jordan motioned to Al and the two of them headed toward the room Brody indicated. The door was open and Jordan knocked softly on the jam so as not to startle the woman.

"Pardon me, ma'am, but I'm Detective Graves and this is Detective Parker. Do you think we could ask you a few questions?"

The woman lifted her hand a few inches and motioned them inside. "You can try, but I don't remember anything. The doctor already asked."

A small smile pulled at Jordan's lips.

"Well, no offense to Dr. Cavanaugh, but he's not a detective, so he might not have asked the right questions." He held out the broken phone. "Do you recognize this?" As the woman looked at it, he assessed her injuries. Her right foot was in a makeshift cast, cuts and bruises covered her right leg and arm, and a bandage wrapped around her head. Though she stared at them with her right eye, the left was purple, blue, and swollen shut. She had definitely taken a beating. It was a miracle she was alive.

A spark of recognition flared in the woman's eye before she shut it again. "That's my phone, isn't it?"

"We pulled it from your car, so we believe it was your phone."

"I was going to use it," she said slowly as if pulling the words from memory, "but it was on the passenger seat and I couldn't reach it, but I can't remember why I was going to use it."

"Unfortunately, it's destroyed and there was no purse or wallet inside the car that we could find. Do you know why you might have been driving without your license?"

She opened her mouth to reply but then paused. Her eye opened again and looked from him to Al and back again. "Am I in trouble, officers?"

He stared at her for a second before the realization of her hesitation made sense. Then he chuckled softly. "For driving without a license? No. You should always carry it and you can be fined for not having it, but we're not here to issue you a ticket. We're more concerned with the accident. Our witness says the black truck hit you, but we aren't sure if the accident was on purpose or not. Do you remember anything?"

"I don't think it was an accident. I can't remember why, but I think someone was after me. Did the witness help at all?"

Al stepped forward, "He wasn't able to supply us with much unfortunately, so we were hoping this phone might jog some memories."

"I wish it did, but I have nothing more."

"That's okay, it will probably come back." Jordan was about to thank her when his phone rang. He pulled it from his pocket and turned away slightly when he recognized Stone's number. "Detective Graves."

"Jordan, are you with the hit and run victim?"

"Yes, sir, we are here now." Did Stone have information?

"Ask her about the name Tia Sweetchild."

Jordan glanced back at the woman. "Tia Sweetchild?"

"Yes, the license plate you ran just came back as a rental car. I called the company and they said a Tia Sweetchild rented the car. The funny thing is, her address is in California, so she's not from here."

Interesting. If she wasn't from Illinois, what was she doing here? "Okay, sir." Jordan hung up the phone and returned to the side of the woman's bed. "Does the name Tia Sweetchild ring a bell for you?"

"Is that me? Am I Tia?" she asked.

"The car you were driving was rented to a Tia Sweetchild so yes, we believe so. However, the address listed on the rental agreement is in California, so we're not sure what you would be doing here in Illinois."

The woman paused, and he wondered what she was thinking. Did the name sound familiar to her? Was she simply pretending not to know? "I have no idea what I was doing here, but now that we know my name, we should be able to find out some more about me, right?"

"We'll certainly do our best," Al said. "If you remember anything else, please call us." She handed Tia a white business card.

"We'll be in touch as soon as we have more information," Jordan said. As they exited the room, he turned to Al. "What do you think?"

"I think she's beat up pretty badly."

"Yeah, but do you think she's telling the truth?"

Al's lips formed a tight line. "I don't know, but something about this case bothers me. I think we better have a look into Tia Sweetchild."

Jordan couldn't agree more.

CHAPTER 3

*J*ordan sighed as he shut down his computer for the night. He had been hoping to find out more about Tia Sweetwater, but other than discovering she was an author of clean romance books, he had come up empty handed. Maybe dinner would help.

He pulled out his cell phone and dialed Cassidy's number. He hadn't had a chance to catch up with her since the accident, and he was missing her company.

"Hey Jordan," she said when the call went through.

"Hey Cassidy. You feel like dinner tonight?"

"I'd love to," she said sighing softly, "but

I'm on shift tonight. Tomorrow though, okay?"

"Sure thing." Jordan shouldn't be upset that Cassidy had work especially since his own job wreaked havoc on their plans a lot of the time as well, but he missed her. The opening of Fire Dreams had kept him busy in the evenings the last few weeks and now there was this hit and run case. Hopefully, things would slow down again soon.

With a sigh, he headed out of the office and to his car. There was a restaurant down the street from his house. He could pick up a dinner and ponder the case as he ate.

The unintelligible hum of conversation assaulted him as Jordan stepped into the dim atmosphere. He scanned the area - a habit he'd had even before becoming a cop - and was surprised to find Brody at the bar. Jordan didn't drink, but he was curious if Tia had remembered anything more.

"You want to open a tab?" the bartender asked Brody.

"No need," Jordan said pulling out a five and placing it on the counter. Brody looked up at him in surprise. "It's on me. Grab that and follow me."

"Were you following me, detective?" Brody asked as he sat in the booth.

"No, but I'm glad I ran into you. Did our patient remember anything more today?"

Brody shook his head. "No, but I didn't really ask today. I did find out she was an author though and I brought in one of her books hoping it would help."

Jordan's eyes narrowed. He hadn't shared the information with Brody yet. "How did you find out she was an author?"

"I had dinner with Nick last night and he recognized her name, so we googled her. Anyway, when I showed her the book, she said she remembered something when she touched it." He paused, as if trying to remember her words. "A man saying 'What are you doing here?' But that was all she could remember. She didn't even remember being an author. Should I be asking specific questions? Did you find something out?"

Jordan blew out an agitated breath. "Not much more than that, but it just isn't sitting well with me. Why would anyone want to harm an author? She's not a big name like Stephen King or J.K Rowling so I don't think it was about money, and she writes clean romance so I doubt she offended someone enough to want to kill her. All I have are questions - the biggest one being what was she doing here in the first place?"

"I don't know." Brody shook his head and took a sip of his beer. "She said a woman visited her today and claimed she was in town for that reason."

Jordan's head snapped forward. "What? She had a visitor?" Why did neither of them tell him about this?

"Yes, she didn't remember the woman, but she hasn't remembered much. Why? Is that a bad thing?"

Agitation filled Jordan. He would never solve this case if they didn't give him all the information. "It could be. We asked her to call us if anything else happened. We need to know everything if we are going to figure this out. I can't believe she didn't tell us she had a visitor. Did you get the woman's name?"

Brody shook his head. "No, sorry, I was a little busy, but I can ask tomorrow."

"I'll go over myself tomorrow to ask, but please, Brody, we can't help if we don't know everything. Even if it seems trivial."

Brody gave a curt nod. "I understand. It seems she gets a few pieces of her memory back every day. Maybe we'll know more in a day or two."

Jordan ran a hand across his chin. "Let's hope that's soon enough, but please keep an eye on her and call me if you learn anything. I just have a bad feeling about all of this."

CHAPTER 4

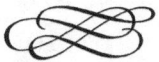

"So, I hear you had a visitor yesterday," Jordan said as he entered Tia's room.

She looked up at him in surprise. "I did. How did you…?"

"I ran into Dr. Cavanaugh last night. I thought we told you to call us."

"You asked me to call you if I remembered anything else. I didn't remember Debra. She said we were friends and brought me my purse."

Jordan sighed as he realized she was right. Next time they would have to be more specific. "Wait, did you say she brought you your purse?"

Tia pointed to the nearby table. "I didn't remember much from it either before you ask.

I remember buying it at a shop, and I remembered attending a movie and what kind of coffee I drink. Nothing that would change the world."

"I'm going to need to examine your purse and its contents," Jordan said plucking the purse from the table.

Tia took a deep breath, and her eye shifted. "I did remember one more thing. Well, at least I think I did."

"What's that?"

"There's a note in the purse with the name Rico Rearden and a time on it. I think I was visiting him and not Debra."

Interesting. "Why would Debra lie about that?"

"I don't know. Maybe I was visiting them both and just remember him?"

Jordan doubted that. More likely Debra was lying about something. The question was what? "Tia, I really need you to call me or have Dr. Cavanaugh contact me if anything else happens. We can't protect you if we don't know everything."

"I understand."

Jordan wasn't sure she did, but he hoped so. There were already enough questions in this case. He didn't need anymore. "I'll bring this back after we process it," he said holding up the purse. "Remember, anything else."

"I promise."

He shook his head as he walked out of her room and back to his car. He loved his job but dealing with a woman who remembered nothing was definitely proving challenging especially if someone was out to get her.

"Nice purse," Al said as he set the bag down on his desk.

He shot her a smirk. "Very funny. It's not mine. It's Tia's. Evidently, a visitor dropped it off to her yesterday. A visitor she neglected to tell us about."

"We better get to work on that name before Stone finds out."

She didn't have to tell Jordan twice. "Okay, you take the name Debra and Rico Rearden. I'm going to go through the bag and see if I can get any fingerprints." While he suspected the only fingerprints he would find would belong to Tia and Debra, he wanted to make sure nothing else slipped past him.

"WAIT, what? Yeah, I'll be right there." Jordan shook his head as he ended the call.

"What was that about?" Al asked.

Jordan sighed and ran his hand across his chin. "Evidently Debra came back to the hospital today. With a gun."

Al's eyes widened. "What?"

"Yeah, she tried to kill Tia. She's claiming Tia was having an affair with Rico, her husband." Jordan shook his head, not sure how this had gone south so quickly. "Stone is going to lose it. Keep digging while I go pick her up. Maybe that will at least help."

Jordan grabbed his keys. He felt like he had just left the hospital and here he was going back once again.

He pulled into the lot and hurried into the hospital heading directly for the security office. Debra Rearden sat with her hands cuffed and resting in her lap. A blank expression rested on her face.

"Has she said anything?" Jordan asked as he signed the paperwork to take custody of Debra.

The security guard shook his head. "Not since we dragged her from the room. She said plenty in the room though. Dr. Cavanaugh wrote up a statement already." He handed it across the table.

Jordan scanned it before folding it and

placing it in his pocket. "Thank you. Can you get a security guard posted outside Tia Sweetchild's room?"

"That might be challenging," the security guard said with an apologetic grin, "we're short staffed as it is."

"Look, station someone there, and I'll see if the police department can help with the cost." He hoped Stone would okay the cost but figured with the attempt on Tia's life that he would find it somehow. Jordan turned to the woman. "Let's go, Debra."

She stared at him with cool eyes, but didn't budge forcing him to haul her up. "You want to tell me why you tried to kill Tia Sweetchild?"

Her answer was a tilt of her chin into the air. Well, Jordan wouldn't push her - Stone would get the information he needed when he took a turn at questioning her.

Debra said nothing on the ride to the station. Nor did she say a word as Jordan processed her and led her toward the holding cell.

"What the heck happened this morning, Jordan?" Stone's angry voice filled the room after Jordan returned from placing Debra in the holding cell.

Jordan shook his head. It wasn't his fault, but Stone didn't often care about fault, he cared about results. "Tia didn't call us when the woman visited yesterday. I found out about her late last night from Brody and went in this morning to talk to her, but we were still running her background."

"Our job is to stay on top of this, not clean up messes."

Jordan nodded and shot a look at Al. She had briefed him on his way back with Debra. "I understand, sir. We've been working since I returned this morning, and we do have some information. Debra Rearden is clean, but she is married to Rico Rearden."

Stone's eyes narrowed. "Rico Rearden? Why does his name sound familiar?"

"Because his name has appeared on a few narcotics searches. So far, they haven't been able to pin anything on him, but they think he might be involved in a drug trafficking ring."

"A drug dealer? What was our amnesic author doing with a drug dealer?"

"We're still working on that," Al said, "but Rico also owns a publishing company – PressBooks, LLC. It's possible Tia didn't know he was a dealer and was meeting with him about a publishing opportunity."

Stone stalked around the board perusing the evidence. "And what about the black truck?"

Jordan shook his head. "No luck on that so far. Rico owns a Mercedes and a Mustang and Debra drives a Firebird. No black truck registered in either of their names."

"So, we have nothing?" Frustration flooded Stone's voice and his eyes as he turned back to them.

"We'll keep digging."

"You do that. I'll talk to Debra," he said as he turned on his heel and stalked out of the room.

CHAPTER 5

Jordan sighed as he headed out of the office for the night. He still didn't have as much information as he would like, but he had promised Graham to help out at Fire Dreams tonight. He didn't really feel like a shift, but a promise was a promise. Surprise flooded him as he pushed open the door and found himself face to face with Brody. "Brody? What are you doing here?"

"I was hoping I could talk to you about Tia and the woman from the hospital earlier."

Jordan looked over his shoulder and then back at Brody. Stone wouldn't care that he filled the doctor in, but there was no need to share where other ears could hear. "Not here.

I'm headed over to Fire Dreams. Meet me there and I'll tell you what I know, but it isn't much."

Ten minutes later they sat in a booth. Jordan had procured a glass of water for each of them along with a basket of chips and persuaded Graham he would only be a minute. Still, the place was hopping having recovered nicely from the spoiled opening a few days before and Jordan kept glancing around realizing he should be helping rather than sitting and talking.

"So, the lady from the hospital is indeed Debra Rearden. If you or Tia had told us about her yesterday, we could have looked into her sooner and possibility avoided the murder attempt. She's clean, but her husband, Rico, has a few questionable connections."

"What kind of questionable connections?" Brody asked.

"On paper, he's the head of a publishing company which might explain the connection to Tia, but we've found some unusual activity with some known drug dealers. Nothing that points to him being directly involved, and Narcotics has never been able to pin anything on him, but we're widening our search to be sure."

Brody nodded and snagged a chip. "Drugs? Really? Tia said she had a meeting with Rico, but she doesn't seem like the type to be into drug deals."

Jordan took a sip of his water. "Maybe she isn't, but I did a little more research on her today. It appears she stayed under the radar. At least recently. Evidently a few months ago, she kind of lost it after trying to damage the reputation of a fellow romance author, Ava McDermott. She sent photos to tabloids and appeared on a few talk shows claiming the relationship Ava was in was a fake one. I don't know why anyone would fake a relationship, but maybe if you are a public figure, it's more important."

Brody nearly choked on his chip. "What? I can't see her doing that."

Jordan shrugged. "Well, maybe the head injury changed her or maybe she changed after the incident. She failed to do much except soil her own reputation. Regardless, it's clear Tia did know Rico. There's no other reason Debra would have come after her. Perhaps she was talking to him about new publishing opportunities. We just don't know any more than that."

"Is there a chance she was having an affair with him as his wife claimed?" Brody asked before taking a drink of his water.

Jordan hadn't found anything pointing to an affair, but there was still so much they didn't know. "That I can't speak to. Yet. But we'll be looking into Rico more." He shook some salt on a chip before stuffing it into his mouth.

"And what about the black truck. Did it belong to Debra?"

Jordan shook his head as he finished chewing. "No, neither she nor her husband appear to own one."

"So, someone might still be after Tia."

"It's possible or it could just be that the accident was just that. An accident."

"But you don't believe that, do you?" Brody asked.

"No, I don't. It's just a gut feeling, but I don't. I've talked with the hospital about posting a security guard outside her door as well." Jordan looked around again and waved at Graham behind the counter area who was shooting him a glare. "I have to help out here, but I promise to keep you in the loop of what we find."

"Thank you," Brody said as Jordan stood.

Jordan nodded and hurried over to Graham. "Sorry, it was about the case."

"It always is," Graham said with a sigh, "but Jordan if we are going to make this restaurant work, I need your help. I need you here mentally as well as physically."

"Got it." This was exactly why Jordan hadn't wanted to open a restaurant. Maybe if the restaurant continued to do well, they could hire more help giving him more time off. Between work and Cassidy, he just didn't have a lot of time to spare.

CHAPTER 6

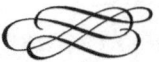

*J*ordan leaned back and rubbed his eyes. He had been staring at the computer screen for hours trying to find out more about Tia and the Reardens, but nothing was popping up. No other connection beside the publishing company, and even that was a guess.

"Coming up empty over there?" Al asked from across the desk.

"Yeah, crickets." Thankfully, Stone had forgotten about the deadline after the attempt on Tia's life, but Jordan was starting to wonder if his gut was wrong and the accident was really just an accident.

Beside him, his cell phone rang. He glanced down surprised to see a number he didn't recognize. "Detective Graves," he said after punching the answer button.

"Jordan? It's Brody. Tia received some flowers this morning, and I think you need to come and see the card."

"The card is suspicious?"

"Yes, I'm going to take her for a short walk, and then we'll be back." Brody's voice remained calm as if he was trying not to scare Tia any more than she already had been.

"I'll be right there."

"Back to the hospital?" Al asked glancing up at him.

"Yes, Brody said Tia received suspicious flowers. I shouldn't be long."

When Jordan arrived at the hospital, he once again declared himself before heading to Tia's room. The flowers were on the table, but an examination of them revealed nothing out of the ordinary. However, the note left by her bed was another matter entirely. There were no words on the card, only a human face with its eyes and mouth sewed shut. It was creepy to say the very least.

"Where do these flowers come from?" he asked when Brody and Tia returned to the room a moment later.

"From the gift shop downstairs usually or

from outside sources," Dr. Cavanaugh said as he wheeled Tia back to the bed.

"And how do they get delivered?"

Dr. Cavanaugh held out his hand and helped Tia stand and get situated back in the bed. "An orderly generally brings them to the floor and then either delivers them or gives them to the nurses to deliver."

"Valerie brought mine in," Tia supplied.

Jordan glanced over at her before turning his attention back to Brody. "I'm going to need to speak with her as well."

"Fine, I'll introduce you." Dr. Cavanaugh turned back to Tia. "I'll check on you before I leave for the night."

Jordan followed Brody out of the room and into the main ICU area. "That's Valerie there, the one with the dark hair," Brody said pointing. "Valerie? Can we have a moment?"

Valerie looked up at them, questions in her eyes, but she made her way over to them.

"The flowers you delivered to Tia Sweetchild this morning. How did they get here?" Jordan asked.

"An orderly brought them up as they do every day. I distributed them to the correct rooms. Why?" Her gaze fluttered from Brody to Jordan and back again.

Jordan shot Brody a silencing look. It would be better to keep the information on the card to as few people as possible. "I just need to investigate the situation a little more. Where is the gift shop?"

"Downstairs," Brody said. "I would show you myself, but I do need to check on the other patients."

"I'm sure I can find it," Jordan said. "Thank you for your help, Valerie."

Jordan left the ICU and headed down to the gift shop. It was a small office-sized room stuffed full of baskets, animals, and balloons.

"Can I help you?"

Jordan looked over to see a young man, probably in his early twenties stand up from behind the small counter. He quickly stashed something in his pocket which Jordan assumed was a cell phone.

"Yes, can you tell me who bought flowers for the woman in ICU room six today?" He pulled back his jacket so he could see the badge on his jeans.

"Um, I'm not sure, but let me look." He tapped the screen on the tablet in front of him and scrolled with his finger. "Sorry, the person paid in cash. We only take names if they pay with cards."

Jordan was not surprised. He hadn't expected the person to leave a paper trail. "Do you happen to remember them?"

The young man had the decency to look chagrined. "I'm sorry; I don't. This is a part-time gig for me, just helping to pay for college."

"Is there a camera that looks into the shop?" Jordan tried to keep his patience with the young man.

He shrugged and dropped his eyes to his lap. "You could check with security, but I just don't know."

"Thank you." Jordan was fairly certain that security would be a dead end as well, but he would be remiss if he didn't at least ask.

The security guard in the office today was not the same one from yesterday, and Jordan wondered briefly how many security guards the hospital employed.

"Can I help you?" the man asked when Jordan entered.

"Detective Jordan Graves. I was hoping to see camera footage that points to the gift shop."

"There is no camera on the gift shop," the security guard said. "We don't have a large enough budget to cover a lot of the areas, so the cameras are only in the high traffic areas - entrances and the like."

Jordan figured as much. After thanking the guard, he returned to the police station to see what progress Al had made.

"Dead end on the flowers?" she asked.

"Yeah, creepy card though." He showed her the image nodding as she grimaced. "I'm going to send it to the lab for prints, but I doubt we'll find any. Whoever this is, they've taken care to not be noticed. Paid cash too. Did you find anything else about Rico and Debra?"

"A little." Her eyes dropped to her computer screen. "Evidently Rico is quite the playboy. He's had a string of women he's paraded around places which explains why his wife was so angry. She probably thought Tia was one of those women. Narcotics said the Chicago office thinks he's involved with some deals there, but they can't prove any yet. They think this publishing company might be a front."

"If we can get this Rico, the Chicago chief would be very grateful," Stone said joining the conversation.

"We'll keep doing our best," Jordan said.

CHAPTER 7

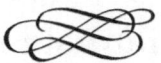

Jordan stopped by the hospital on his way home in hopes of catching Brody on his way out. Until he was sure Tia was innocent, he felt safer sharing his intel with Brody and letting him decide how much to pass on. He obviously had a better idea of who Tia was since he saw her every day.

"Detective, did you find out anything more about the flowers?" Brody asked as he approached.

Jordan pushed himself off Brody's car and glanced around the empty lot. "Unfortunately not. They *were* purchased at the gift shop here, but paid for in cash. The clerk couldn't remember who purchased them and there's no camera that points that direction. We do have some new intel though. It appears Rico Rearden may be involved in drug trafficking over in Chicago. He didn't come up on our initial radar because he doesn't deal here, but it looks like he might hold meetings here and use his publishing business as a front."

"Do you think Tia was helping him move drugs?" Emotions struggled across Brody's face as if he didn't want to believe Tia could be involved in criminal behavior.

While Jordan didn't believe Tia was a criminal, he had worked on the force long enough to know that sometimes people weren't as they seemed. "We don't know what to think. It's possible she was involved though nothing in her background suggests it. It's more probable she was there for the meeting she had scheduled and may have stumbled across a secret meeting. Either way, we need to keep a close eye on her. She may not be as innocent as we think."

Brody shook his head. "Okay, thanks Jordan, I'll do my best."

Jordan nodded and returned to his car. He had another late shift tonight at Fire Dreams, but Cassidy had promised to stop by after her shift and he was looking forward to seeing her. He felt like he hadn't seen her in days.

"Well, I didn't think I'd beat you in here," she said with a smile as he stepped behind the counter area. The restaurant didn't serve alcohol, but he and Graham had wanted a counter area where people could sit and be served quickly.

He leaned in and placed a quick kiss on her lips. "I'm sure glad you did. How was work?"

"Slow thankfully," she said. As a firefighter, her job was a lot like his, nicer when it was slow. "I cleaned the truck today, broke up a bickering argument between Luca and Deacon and avoided kitchen duty, so all in all, a good day."

"That's good. I'm glad to hear it. When this case gets settled, how about we plan a movie night."

She smiled at him. "That sounds delicious, Detective Graves. So, how is your case coming along? How is the woman?"

Jordan glanced around to make sure no one else was listening to their conversation, but thankfully tonight the counter area was slow. Most of the patrons had chosen booths or tables out in the main restaurant and Cassidy was the sole patron at the counter.

"She is recovering though she has memory loss. Someone's already tried to kill her, and I don't think the accident was an accident. I just worry something worse is going to happen, but I can't be at the hospital all day to protect her either. I asked for a security guard for her, but I worry that it still isn't enough."

Cassidy laid a hand on his arm. "I am sure you are doing all that you can."

He hoped so, but if he was, why did it still seem as if it wasn't enough?

CHAPTER 8

*J*ordan sighed as the fingerprint report came across his computer. Nothing. Just as he'd expected. This case was a plethora of questions with no answers.

"Nothing?" Al asked.

"No fingerprints," Jordan said as his phone rang. He pulled it out and punched the answer call button. "Detective Graves."

"Jordan? It's Brody Cavanaugh at Fire Beach Hospital. We are in lockdown. A code silver was reported a few moments ago in the ICU. I am locked in the bathroom in room six with Tia."

Jordan sucked in his breath surprised at

how calm Brody sounded. "I'm on my way. Do you know what the weapon is?"

"No, I haven't seen anything. I locked the door per protocol as soon as the announcement was made."

"Understood. I'm going to transfer you to a dispatch operator and I want you to stay on the line until I get there."

"I'll try, but we're in the bathroom and I only had two bars. I don't know if they'll hold….."

"Brody? Brody?" Jordan held the phone out and looked at the screen. "Grab your stuff, Al. We need to get to the hospital."

"What's going on?" Stone asked entering the room.

"Brody just called. There's a cold silver at the hospital."

"Go," he said with a wave of his hand.

Jordan rushed out of the room with Al close on his heels.

"Do we even know what we're getting into?" Al asked as they climbed into his car.

"I'm not sure. Brody couldn't see the weapon or the perpetrator, so we go in carefully, and we check with security first. Hopefully, they put someone outside her room." He flicked the button to turn on the lights and siren and pressed his foot on the accelerator.

The parking lot looked no different when they arrived, and Jordan wondered how they handled Code Silvers. Did everyone lock down in individual rooms as Brody did? Or was there another procedure for other areas? He realized he had no idea, and he probably should. After this case, he would familiarize himself with the hospital's procedures.

The main hospital entrance opened for them, but the security guard there accosted them before they got very far. "Are you here about the Code Silver?"

"We are. Do we need to do anything special?"

The security guard shook his head. "Tom is covering the door from inside. I'll radio him when we get there to let you in."

Jordan and Al followed the security guard, whose nametag read Roger, down the hall to the ICU. The doors were indeed locked, but after a quick conversation with the guard inside, the door opened and the security guard ushered them in. Jordan scanned the area as he stepped in.

Most of the patient room doors were closed. A doctor, a nurse, and another security guard hovered around a patient who held a scalpel in his hands. Was this the code silver?

Cautiously, he and Al approached the small group. "Is there anything we can do to help?" Jordan asked.

At the sound of his voice, the patient turned to look at Jordan, and the nurse jammed a syringe in his arm. The patient cried out in surprise or pain, Jordan wasn't sure which, but he dropped the scalpel and folded to the floor.

"Looks like you already did," the doctor said. "Thank you."

"Was that it? That was the Code Silver?" Al asked.

The doctor turned confused eyes on her. "Did you want it to be worse?"

"No," Jordan said jumping in, "It's just we received a call from Dr. Cavanaugh. Since there had already been an attempt on his patient's life, we assumed it was another one."

"Thankfully not. We'll make the announcement that the Code Silver is lifted, but you can go rescue Dr. Cavanaugh now," the nurse said.

Jordan wasted no time. He hurried over to Tia's room, but the door was locked. "Dr.

Cavanaugh," he hollered pounding on the door, "you can open up."

Al tapped him on the shoulder to grab his attention. "Hold on there, Hulk. Let me get the key."

Jordan watched her walk over to the nurse and return with the woman a moment later. The nurse produced a master key from her pocket and opened the room for him. Silence greeted them, and Jordan wondered if there had been more to the Code Silver that maybe the doctor and nurse didn't know about.

Then he remembered Brody stating they were hiding in the bathroom. He crossed the room in three strides and pounded on the bathroom door. "Dr. Cavanaugh? Open up. It's Detective Graves."

A moment later the lock clicked and the door opened. Tia lay in the bathtub with her injured ankle propped up on the side and both she and Brody blinked against the bright lights.

"Is it safe to come out then?" Brody asked.

"It is," Jordan said, "Evidently, it was a patient who suffered a psychiatric break and grabbed a scalpel off a tray."

"I'm sorry," Brody said, "after our conversation-"

"You were right to do what you did," Jordan assured him. "We still haven't found the driver of the black truck or who sent Tia those flowers and what you did made perfect sense. However, unless you need further assistance, we'll get back to work on finding the suspects."

"Wait Detective Graves?" Jordan turned to Tia and waited. "I remembered more. I was there to see Rico about a publishing opportunity, but I turned it down when I found out he was married and looking for an affair. He kicked me out, but I had forgotten my purse. When I returned, he shoved me in a closet. I heard men's voices arguing, and I thought perhaps they were reporters out for a story on me which is why I ran when I did."

"Did you see any of the men? Do you remember anything about them?"

"Not their faces. When I stepped out of the closet, I looked left. They were on the balcony, but it was dark outside. I couldn't see their faces, but I felt the icy hatred in their gaze when they saw me. I didn't think they had followed me at first, but then lights blinded me on the road. I slowed down thinking maybe it was just teenagers out for a joy ride, but when they didn't pass me, I figured they had followed me after all. Then the truck hit me."

Jordan's face hardened and he exchanged a glance with Brody. "Okay, thank you, Tia. We'll look into all of this and let you know what we find. Do the two of you need anything else?"

"I think we'll be fine," Brody said. The look he flashed Tia held more than concern, and Jordan wondered if a relationship might bloom between the two of them.

"Do you think we're looking for two cars then?" Al asked as they exited the room.

Jordan shook his head. "I have no idea, but I suppose we have to assume so. Everything we learn about this case just brings more questions."

"That's true, but we haven't even found the black truck yet. How do we find a second vehicle when we have no idea what it was?"

Jordan didn't know. He just didn't know.

CHAPTER 9

*J*ordan had just pulled into the parking lot of the police station when his phone rang again. His eyes widened as he looked at the number. "It's Brody. Again."

"What? We just left."

Jordan nodded at her and then answered the phone. "Brody? What's going on?"

"Sorry to bother you, Jordan, but Tia just informed me she had a new nurse yesterday."

"Okay, I'm not following," Jordan said.

"I didn't assign a new nurse. Maybe it's nothing, but it's the second time I've heard about this new nurse. One of our volunteers told me a new nurse tried to keep her from reading to the patients the other day, and Tia confirmed it was the same woman."

With any other case, Jordan might consider this information innocuous, but he wasn't going to count anything out in this case. "I'll be right there."

He ended the call and turned to Al. "Go tell Stone what we've found. Brody says there's a woman I need to check into – might be nothing but definitely suspicious."

"Be sure and watch your back," Al said as she stepped out of the car.

"Always do," Jordan said before she shut the door. Then he pointed the car back to the hospital.

"So, TELL ME ABOUT THIS WOMAN," Jordan said when he was back in Tia's room.

"She's got shoulder length dark hair, olive skin, and brown eyes. She wasn't wearing a name tag when she came in, so I don't know what name she is going by, but she looks young. Under thirty probably," Tia said.

"All right, we'll inform the guard to let no one in," Jordan began.

"We need to allow one nurse," Brody said, "to check on Tia if necessary."

"Okay, one nurse, but no one else," Jordan agreed though it didn't sit well with him. "Not until we find this woman and get her story."

"Agreed. Sit tight, Tia. We'll be back soon."

Even Brody's words didn't erase the apprehensive look from Tia's face, but she agreed.

After a quick stop to inform the security guard not to allow anyone but Sophie into the room, Jordan and Brody set off in search of the mystery woman. Jordan wished they had a picture of the woman, but Tia couldn't travel quickly enough and the volunteer wasn't at the hospital.

They started in the ICU first, but after a glance into every patient room and the break room, no dark-haired unknown nurse appeared.

"Where to next?" Jordan asked. Brody was much more familiar with the hospital than he was.

"Let's check the surrounding areas and their break rooms. If she's after Tia, I doubt she will wander too far from ICU."

They moved to the department closest to

ICU, but it did not reveal the woman in question either. However, as they turned the corner to the break room, a dark-haired woman exited and headed away from them.

"Stop," Jordan called.

The woman glanced back at them, and her eyes widened before she took off running down the hall. Jordan bolted after her, turning his head just long enough to holler back to Brody, "Go check on Tia."

As he ran, he grabbed his phone and punched the number to reach Al. "Al, get over to the hospital and bring backup." He hung up before she could ask questions and shoved the phone back in his pocket. The woman was fast, and she had just burst through the stairwell door. He pushed it open behind her, hoping the woman wasn't carrying a gun. She looked up as the door opened, and it caused her to miss a step. She stumbled down the last two, falling into the wall and allowing Jordan to catch up with her.

"You're under arrest," he said pulling her hands behind her back and slapping on a pair of handcuffs. "Want to tell my why you ran?"

She shot him an icy glare but pulled her mouth into a tight line.

"Fine. You'll talk to us soon, although

anything you say can and will be used against you in a court of law. You have the right to an attorney. If you cannot afford an attorney, one will be appointed for you." He continued spouting the Miranda rights as he led her back toward ICU.

"Detective Graves, we have another one for you," the security guard said as Jordan entered the ICU.

"Another one?"

"Yes, a man tried to take out Tia's security guard and then her with a syringe full of insulin. Thankfully Dr. Cavanaugh arrived in time. They are both recovering."

Jordan shook his head. How had this gotten so crazy so fast? "Where is he?"

"In the security office," the man said, "waiting for you."

Al and Stone appeared before Jordan could head that direction, and he filled them in.

"Let's pick him up and get them processed," Stone said taking charge of the unknown woman.

Jordan pulled out his phone when they reached the security office and snapped a picture of both the man and the woman. "I'll meet you guys back at the station. I'm going to see if our clerk can identify either of these two."

Stone nodded and Jordan headed back toward the gift shop. Relief filled him when he found the same young man from earlier still behind the counter. He wasn't sure what the hours of the gift shop were or how long his shift was, but God was on his side today.

"Hey, remember me?" he asked as he approached the counter.

He looked up, stashing his phone under some papers. "Yeah, sure, what can I do for you?"

"I want to show you two photos and see if either of these people might be the ones who bought flowers for room six."

"Okay, I can try."

Jordan pulled up the picture of the man and then turned his phone toward the clerk. He scrunched his eyes at it but shook his head.

"Sorry, he doesn't look familiar."

"All right, how about her?" He flicked to the picture of the woman and repeated the process.

The clerk nodded. "Yeah, she looks familiar. Only she wasn't wearing a nurse's uniform. I would have remembered that."

"Thank you. You've been very helpful,"

Jordan said before exiting the gift shop. Whoever the woman was, she was involved in this case somehow.

"I'VE GOT NAMES," Al said, a note of triumph in her voice. She stood and walked over to the white board. "Meet Adrian and Susanna Petrov." Al scribbled the names quickly above the pictures. "Adrian Petrov is the leader of a large gang in Chicago and Narcotics believes he is the head of a drug organization."

"I've got an address too," Jordan added as his computer pulled up the information. "233 Palisades Drive. Oh, and guess what Adrian drives?"

"I'm going to go out on a limb and say a black truck," Stone supplied. "Okay, you two go check out the place. Take Albright and Givens with you. I'll stay here and see what I can get from the Petrovs."

The four cops nodded at each other and headed out. Jordan was beginning to feel as if he spent more time on the road than at his desk lately.

233 Palisades Drive was a large two-story house on the outskirts of town. Jordan

doubted they would meet resistance, but they went out with guns drawn anyway. They didn't have a search warrant yet, but the garage had windows and the view inside revealed a black Ford truck. Enough probable cause for a closer look.

Albright got the side door opened and they stepped inside. "I'd say this is your vehicle."

Jordan stared at the dented front end and smiled. Adrian had obviously tried to have it fixed, but there was enough damage and a few conspicuous flecks of red paint remaining that he was sure this was the vehicle they were looking for. He'd finally be able to tell Tia it was over.

"How are you two doing?" Jordan asked as he entered Tia's room an hour later.

They turned fear-filled eyes on him. "Did you get the guy?" Brody asked. "Who was he?"

Jordan nodded. "We did. His name is Adrian Petrov. He's the leader of one of the bigger gangs out of Chicago and the head of a drug organization. He isn't saying much right now, but Stone will take care of that. We did manage to ascertain his address." He turned to Tia and a slight smile pulled at his lips, "Where we found a black Ford truck, and though he tried to have it fixed, we are almost certain it was the same truck that hit you. It's over, Tia."

"That's wonderful." Brody turned to Tia, and a broad grin graced his features.

Tia forced a smile in return, but it was still riddled with worry. "Wait, what about the nurse?"

"We got her too. Susanna Petrov, his wife. She's not talking either, but from what we can gather, they obtained uniforms when they saw on the news that you were in ICU. We're not sure whether she was merely keeping him informed or if she was a backup plan, but we do know that she's the one who bought the flowers. I showed pictures to the clerk at the gift shop, and he was able to ID her."

"What about Rico?"

Jordan's jaw clenched and his eyes shifted just slightly. Rico was the one missing link. "He's in the wind. We think he's in Chicago hiding out and trying to clean up this mess, but I promise you, we're still looking for him."

"Thank you, Detective Graves."

"Call me Jordan," he said as he held her gaze.

"Yes, thank you, Jordan," Brody said clapping a hand on Jordan's shoulder before turning back to Tia. "We need to monitor you to be sure the insulin didn't damage anything, but if all goes well, and as long as your fever is still gone, you might be able to leave the hospital tomorrow."

She should be glad, but the expression on her face looked anything but. Jordan stepped forward hoping to ease her unease. "I know this is a lot to deal with, Tia. If you'd like to stay in town a little longer, I can find you a temporary place and set you up with a counselor who might be able to work through some of the trauma with you."

Tia smiled up at him. "Thank you, I might take you up on that."

"And I don't know how your recovery will be, but I own a restaurant. I have a need for a good hostess if your doctor says it's okay."

Brody nodded. "I'd be okay with it as long as she can stay off her leg. It would be great if you stayed in town, and I was able to check up on you as well."

"Thank you, Jordan. I think I'll spend

tonight thinking about where I see my life going from here, and I'll let you know."

"You do that." He pulled a card from his pocket and handed it to her. "I know Al gave you a card the first day we were here, but this one has my personal cell. You call me if you want some help. I'm sorry this happened to you, but you are strong. You will be okay."

"Hey, I thought you were going to focus on a movie night with me now that the case is over," Cassidy said laying a hand on his arm. They were sitting on the couch, but Jordan had no idea what the movie on the television was about. His mind was still on Tia.

"Almost over," Jordan said. "Rico Rearden is still out there somewhere."

"And you'll find him," Cassidy said. "You always do."

Jordan smiled at his girlfriend and opened his arm for her to curl into. "What did I do to deserve you?"

"Well, saved me from a stalker for one," she said before placing a kiss on his lips, "but you're an amazing man and probably would have won me regardless."

"I just wish there was more I could do for Tia. She's going to be released tomorrow, and I can still see the fear in her eyes. I just wish I could give her more assurance."

"She's being released tomorrow?" Cassidy asked.

Jordan heard the tone in her voice and glanced down at her. "Yeah, why? What's going on in that pretty head of yours?"

"Well, I can't help with easing her fear, but I do know something that would be good to do."

"What's that?"

"She hasn't had any visitors, right? Not friends anyway."

"No." What was Cassidy getting at.

"So, she's been in the hospital gown the whole time, right?"

Jordan shrugged. "I guess so."

"Well, she can't go home in a hospital gown, so how about we get her some clothes?"

As her words sunk in, Jordan's lips pulled into a wide smile, and he kissed Cassidy again. "You're amazing. Why didn't I think of that?"

"Probably because you're not a girl,"

Cassidy said swatting his chest playfully. "Now, we just need her size."

Jordan's face fell. He had no idea what her size was or how to tell. "How do we do that?"

Cassidy chuckled and moved out of his arms to stand before him. "Is she about my size? Larger? Smaller?"

Jordan had never seen Tia standing but he guessed she was a few inches shorter and a little smaller. "Smaller but not by much and a little shorter."

"See? Was that so hard? We'll pick up some outfits with elastic waists one and two sizes smaller than me. Something is bound to fit. At least until she can purchase more herself."

Jordan stood and wrapped his arms around Cassidy. "You, Cassidy Marcel, are one in a million, you know that?"

She smiled up at him as her arms moved to his neck. "I do, but I certainly don't mind hearing it again."

Jordan chuckled as he leaned down to place his lips on hers. He still couldn't believe his luck in finding Cassidy, and he would tell her every day if that's what it took to keep her in his life.

CHAPTER 11

*J*ordan knocked on Tia's doorframe before entering the next morning. "Brody said you could use a lift."

"Yeah, I could. Plus, I thought I'd take you up on your offer for a place to stay and a job. I'd like to stay in town a little longer."

Jordan was glad to hear and the corners of his lips twitched as he entered and set the bag beside her on the bed. "Would that have anything to do with a handsome doctor by chance?"

"It might," she said, "but I also don't know if there's much to go back to in California. I feel like I can start over here except...."

"Except what?"

Tia sighed and shook her head. "I had a dream last night that someone is still after me. I'm sure it was due to the activity yesterday, but do you think there's any chance that it might be true?"

Jordan ran a hand across his chin wishing he could allay her fears. "I'd be lying if I said no. I do think we got the main people involved, but there's always the chance that someone else decides to seek retribution. If it makes you feel better, the lady who runs the house I'm taking you to is former military. She'll keep an eye on you."

"Did you get any news on Rico?"

He shook his head. "Sorry, we're checking with the PD in Chicago, but it's going to take some time."

"Thanks Jordan."

"You're welcome. Now, in that bag are some clothes and shoes. My girlfriend Cassidy deduced that you had none here. She picked them out, but I had to guess on your size so don't blame her if they're off. She did grab some things with drawstrings so the size shouldn't matter too much."

Tia's fingers touched the bag, and her voice was quiet and full of emotion when she spoke again. "Thank you, Jordan, and tell Cassidy thank you."

He nodded, embarrassed and took a step back. "I'll give you a chance to change and see about getting a wheelchair so we can get you out of here."

He shut the door behind him and turned to the main ICU desk. "How can I get a wheelchair for Tia Sweetchild? She's checking out."

"I'll order you one right away sir," the nurse said as she picked up a phone. "Can I get a wheelchair to ICU? Thank you." She smiled at Jordan as she replaced the phone. "It will be just a minute."

Jordan nodded and waited for the orderly to arrive with the chair. When he finally came around the corner, Jordan took the chair and returned to Tia's door. He knocked lightly. "It's Jordan. Can I come in?"

"Yes, come on in."

"Hey, looking good," he said as he wheeled a chair in. She had managed to get on a stretchy pair of pants and a shirt and neither appeared to be swimming on her. He'd have to tell Cassidy she did a wonderful job in choosing the outfits. "You about ready?

I just got called back to work, so I'm afraid I'll have to drop you and run."

"That's fine, Jordan. Really, you've done so much for me."

Jordan could hear the emotion in her voice, and he wished he could do more. He wished he could assure her she was safe, but while he couldn't do that, he was going to do the next best thing.

He was taking Tia to Cara Hunter's house. Though technically a bed and breakfast, Cara specialized in helping people who needed to get back on their feet or extra protection. Former military, Cara had never completely adjusted to civilian life and was always willing to help out. Cara was as close as Jordan could get to having someone protect Tia twenty-four seven.

Jordan parked the car in front of a weathered-looking rambler close to the beach. The yellow paint was faded but still cheery. "Sorry, it's not much to look at on the outside, but Cara takes good care of the inside."

"It's fine," Tia said. "Hopefully, I don't have to inconvenience her too long."

Jordan touched her arm. "It's no inconvenience. We take care of each other here."

Tia smiled and thanked him, but it was a small smile. Jordan hoped one day he would see a genuine smile on her face.

"Come on, I'll introduce you and help you get settled before I jet back to work."

He turned the engine off and walked around to Tia's side. Before helping her out, he grabbed her crutches out of the back seat, handed them to her, and made sure she was stable. Only then did he grab her bag.

Jordan led the way up the short walk and pushed open the door without knocking. Cara had told him long ago he was welcome anytime. "Cara? It's Jordan and Tia, the woman I told you about."

A woman with short spiky hair appeared in the doorway. Trim and athletic, Cara looked as if she could tangle with the boys any day with her broad shoulders and bold arm definition. "Jordan, good to see you again." She extended a hand in greeting.

Jordan shook her hand and then turned to Tia. "This is Tia. She's recovering from memory loss and a few attempts on her life. She's going to need some help getting back on her feet."

Cara extended her hand to Tia. "It's a

pleasure to meet you, and any friend of Jordan's is welcome here as long as needed."

Tia shook the woman's hand and returned the smile. "Thank you. I appreciate it."

Jordan wished he could stay until he made sure Tia was situated, but duty called. "I hate to run, but I have to get to work. Cara will take good care of you, but please call me if you need anything." Jordan squeezed her shoulder before dropping her bag and exiting out the front door.

CHAPTER 12

*J*ordan's phone rang as he sat down for dinner across from Cassidy. It was Cara's number, but she rarely called him. A feeling of dread spread through him as he answered the phone.

"Cara? Is everything okay?" Across from him, Cassidy set down her fork and fixed questioning eyes on him.

"Jordan?" The woman's voice was a hoarse whisper, but even so he could tell this was Tia on the other end and not Cara.

"Tia? What's wrong?"

"I'm at Cara's, but someone's here. The electricity just went off. Cara sent me to the closet to call you."

Jordan heard an intake of breath and then

the muffled sounds of a man's voice followed by a scream and then silence.

"Tia? Tia?"

"What is it?" Cassidy asked.

"Trouble. Sorry, I have to run." He placed a quick kiss on her lips before grabbing his keys and gun. "I promise I'll make it up to you."

"I know you will. Be safe," she called after him.

Jordan flashed her a wink, but he was already dialing Stone's number as he stepped into the cool night air. "Sir, there's trouble over at Cara's. Can you send everyone?"

Jordan put the lights on but left the siren off as he drove through the city streets. When he reached Cara's street, he turned the lights off as well and coasted to a stop a few doors down. Stone, Al, and Albright pulled up just after him. Jordan wondered briefly where Givens was, but he knew the man lived farther away.

"What do we have?" Stone asked as they consulted together.

"At least one unknown assailant in the house," Jordan said. "I have to assume from the phone call he has Tia. I'm not sure where

Cara is, but she'll be an asset if she's uninjured."

"All right. We go in with signals only. We don't want to give away our position in case there's more than one."

The group nodded and Jordan led the way into the darkened house. No sound came from the front entrance way, but he could hear voices down the hall toward the living room. He motioned to the officers behind him before continuing down the hall.

When they reached the living room, he stopped short. Even in the dim light, he could see that Cara had already taken care of things. Rico Rearden lay on the ground, his hands zip tied together. Brody sat a few feet away next to Tia. Blood ran from his head and Jordan assumed Rico had jumped him either before continuing into the house or before he found Tia. Tia appeared scared but otherwise unharmed.

"I'll call for a bus," Al said as she made her way to Brody and Tia.

Stone and Albright hauled Rico up and led him out of the house as Jordan crossed to Cara who was rubbing her arms. Jordan knew her well enough to know she must have overpowered Rico somehow, possibly a choke hold. He was aware of her college nickname 'The Leech.' "Thank you. I knew you were the right woman for the job."

She shot him a glare as she massaged her forearms. "Next time, a little warning of what I might be facing would be nice."

"I would have warned you except we didn't know what to expect. We thought it was over after the attempt at the hospital, but we didn't realize Rico was not just the front for the organization - he was the head."

"Yeah, we know," Cara said, "He had a hard time keeping his mouth shut. At least while he had the gun on Tia."

"Does that mean it's really over now?" Tia asked.

"It does. Rico's going away for a long time along with his wife and the Petrovs. You may have to testify, but we all owe you a debt of gratitude. I know it wasn't your intent, but through your actions, you've managed to help us take down a pretty large drug organization."

Brody smiled and squeezed Tia's shoulder. "See? I told you everything happens for a reason. I think you've just made up for a lot of the mistakes in your past."

Jordan smiled at the couple. He had a

feeling this would bond them together allowing them to survive anything thrown at them in the future. As for himself, he was glad to mark this case complete. With Rico in custody, all the known players were accounted for and Jordan believed they could finally call this one done.

If you'd like to know the rest of Tia and Brody's story, be sure to read Lost Memories and New Beginnings to hear this story from their point of view. And if you'd like to read more about Jordan and Cassidy, pick up Fire Games, the first book in The Men of Fire Beach series!

IT'S NOT QUITE THE END!

✿

Thank you so much for reading *Lost Memories*. This book was inspired by one of my readers who reached out to me after reading The Producer's Unlikely Bride and told me Tia needed her own story. I had never planned a story for Tia, but I was so touched by her connection to the character that I had to do it. As I've always wanted to attempt an amnesia book, I figured Tia's story was the perfect opportunity, but boy was it harder than I thought.

I hope you enjoyed the story as I really enjoyed writing it. If you did, would you do me a favor? If you did, please leave a review. It really helps. It doesn't have to be long - just a few words to help other readers know what they're getting.

I'd love to hear from you, not only about this story, but about the characters or stories you'd like read in the future. I'm always looking for new ideas and if I use one of your characters or stories, I'll send you a free ebook and paperback of the book with a special dedication. Write to me at loranahoopes@gmail.com. And if you'd like to see what's coming next, be sure to stop by authorloranahoopes.com

I also have a weekly newsletter that contains many wonderful things like pictures of my adorable children, chances to win awesome prizes, new releases and sales I might be holding, great books from other authors, and anything else that strikes my fancy and that I think you would enjoy. I'll even send you the first chapter of my newest (maybe not even released yet) book if you'd like to sign up.

Even better, I solemnly swear to only send out one newsletter a week (usually on Tuesday unless life gets in the way which with three kids it usually does). I will not spam you, sell your email address to solicitors or anyone else, or any of those other terrible things.

God Bless,
    Lorana

NOT READY TO SAY GOODBYE YET?

CASSIDY, Jordan, Brody, and Tia will appear in future books, but I had so many readers reach out to me wanting Bubba's story that I had to do it next!

Never Forget the Past

He's a fireman with a past different from what he claims...

She's a part of that past...

Will he be dragged back into the past he's tried so hard to get away from?

A FREE STORY FOR YOU

ENJOYED THIS STORY? Not ready to quit reading yet? If you sign up for my newsletter, you will receive The Billionaire's Impromptu Bet right away as my thank you gift for choosing to hang out with me.

The Billionaire's Impromptu Bet

A SWAT officer. A bored billionaire heiress. A bet that could change everything....

Read on for a taste of The Billionaire's Impromptu Bet....

THE BILLIONAIRE'S
IMPROMPTU BET PREVIEW

*B*rie Carter fell back spread eagle on her queen-sized canopy bed sending her blonde hair fanning out behind her. With a large sigh, she uttered, "I'm bored."

"How can you be bored? You have like millions of dollars." Her friend, Ariel, plopped down in a seated position on the bed beside her and flicked her raven hair off her shoulder. "You want to go shopping? I hear Tiffany's is having a special right now."

Brie rolled her eyes. Shopping? Where was the excitement in that? With her three platinum cards, she could go shopping whenever she wanted. "No, I'm bored with shopping too. I have everything. I want to do something exciting. Something we don't normally do."

Brie enjoyed being rich. She loved the unlimited credit cards at her disposal, the constant apparel of new clothes, and of course the penthouse apartment her father paid for, but lately, she longed for something more fulfilling.

Ariel's hazel eyes widened. "I know. There's a new bar down on Franklin Street. Why don't we go play a little game?"

Brie sat up, intrigued at the secrecy and the twinkle in Ariel's eyes. "What kind of game?"

"A betting game. You let me pick out any man in the place. Then you try to get him to propose to you."

Brie wrinkled her nose. "But I don't want to get married." She loved her freedom and didn't want to share her penthouse with anyone, especially some man.

"You don't marry him, silly. You just get him to propose."

Brie bit her lip as she thought. It had been awhile since her last relationship and having a man dote on her for a month might be interesting, but…. "I don't know. It doesn't seem very nice."

"How about I sweeten the pot? If you win, I'll set you up on a date with my brother."

Brie cocked her head. Was she serious? The only thing Brie couldn't seem to buy in the world was the affection of Ariel's very handsome, very wealthy, brother. He was a movie star, just the kind of person Brie could consider marrying in the future. She'd had a crush on him as long as she and Ariel had been friends, but he'd always seen her as just that, his little sister's friend. "I thought you didn't want me dating your brother."

"I don't." Ariel shrugged. "But he's between girlfriends right now, and I know you've wanted it for ages. If you win this bet, I'll set you up. I can't guarantee any more than one date though. The rest will be up to you."

Brie wasn't worried about that. Charm she possessed in abundance. She simply needed some alone time with him, and she was certain she'd be able to convince him they were meant to be together. "All right. You've got a deal."

Ariel smiled. "Perfect. Let's get you changed then and see who the lucky man will be.

A tiny tug pulled on Brie's heart that this still wasn't right, but she dismissed it. This was simply a means to an end, and he'd never have to know.

❧

JESSE CALHOUN RELAXED as the rhythmic thudding of the speed bag reached his ears. Though he loved his job, it was stressful being the SWAT sniper. He hated having to take human lives and today had been especially rough. The team had been called out to a drug bust, and Jesse was forced to return fire at three hostiles. He didn't care that they fired at his team and himself first. Taking a life was always hard, and every one of them haunted his dreams.

"You gonna bust that one too?" His co-worker Brendan appeared by his side. Brendan was the opposite of Jesse in nearly every way. Where Jesse's hair was a dark copper, Brendan's was nearly black. Jesse sported paler skin and a dusting of freckles across his nose, but Brendan's skin was naturally dark and freckle free.

Jesse flashed a crooked grin, but kept his eyes on the small, swinging black bag. The speed bag was his way to release, but a few times he had started hitting while still too keyed up and he had ruptured the bag. Okay, five times, but who was counting really? Besides, it was a better way to calm his nerves than other things he could choose. Drinking, fights, gambling, women.

"Nah, I think this one will last a little longer." His shoulders began to burn, and he gave the bag another few punches for good measure before dropping his arms and letting it swing to a stop. "See? It lives to be hit at least another day." Every once in a while, Jesse missed training the way he used to. Before he joined the force, he had been an amateur boxer, on his way to being a pro, but a shoulder injury had delayed his training and forced him to consider something else. It had eventually healed, but by then he had lost his edge.

"Hey, why don't you come drink with us?" Brendan clapped a hand on Jesse's shoulder as they headed into the locker room.

"You know I don't drink." Jesse often felt like the outsider of the team. While half of the six-man team was married, the other half found solace in empty bottles and meaningless relationships. Jesse understood that - their job was such that they never knew if they would come home night after night - but he still couldn't partake.

Brendan opened his locker and pulled out a clean shirt. He peeled off his current one and added deodorant before tugging on the new one. "You don't have to drink. Look, I won't drink either. Just come and hang out with us. You have no one waiting for you at home."

That wasn't entirely true. Jesse had Bugsy, his Boston Terrier, but he understood Brendan's point. Most days, Jesse went home, fed Bugsy, made dinner, and fell asleep watching TV on the couch. It wasn't much of a life. "All right, I'll go, but I'm not drinking."

Brendan's lips pulled back to reveal his perfectly white teeth. He bragged about them, but Jesse knew they were veneers. "That's the spirit. Hurry up and change. We don't want to leave the rest of the team waiting."

"Is everyone coming?" Jesse pulled out his shower necessities. Brendan might feel comfortable going out with just a new application of deodorant, but Jesse needed to wash more than just dirt and sweat off. He needed to wash the sound of the bullets and the sight of lifeless bodies from his mind.

"Yeah, Pat's wife is pregnant again and demanding some crazy food concoctions. Pat agreed to pick them up if she let him have an hour. Cam and Jared's wives are having a girls' night, so the whole gang can be together. It will be nice to hang out when we aren't worried about being shot at."

"Fine. Give me ten minutes. Unlike you, I like to clean up before I go out."

Brendan smirked. "I've never had any complaints. Besides, do you know how long it takes me to get my hair like this?"

Jesse shook his head as he walked into the shower, but he knew it was true. Brendan had rugged good looks and muscles to match. He rarely had a hard time finding a woman. Jesse on the other hand hadn't dated anyone in the last few months. It wasn't that he hadn't been looking, but he was quieter than his teammates. And he wasn't looking for right now. He was looking for forever. He just hadn't found it yet.

Click here to continue reading The Billionaire's Impromptu Bet.

THE STORY DOESN'T END!

You've met a few people and fallen in love....

I bet you're wondering how you can meet everyone else.

Star Lake Series:

When Love Returns: The first in the Star Lake series. Presley Hays and Brandon Scott were best friends in High School until Morgan entered their town and stole Brandon's heart. Devastated, Presley takes a scholarship to Le Cordon Bleu, but five years later, she is back in Star Lake after a tough breakup. Brandon thought he'd never return to Star Lake after Morgan left him and his daughter Joy, but when his father needs help, he returns home and finds more than he

294 | THE STORY DOESN'T END!

bargained for. Can Presley and Brandon forget past hurts or will their stubborn natures keep them apart forever?

Once Upon a Star: The second book in the Star Lake series. Audrey left Star Lake to pursue acting, but after an unplanned pregnancy her jobs and her money dwindled, leaving her no option except to return home and start over. Blake was the quintessential nerd in high school and was never able to tell Audrey how he felt. Now that he's gained confidence and some muscle, will he finally be able to reveal his feelings? Once Upon a Star will take you back to Christmas in Star Lake. Revisit your favorite characters and meet a few ones in this sweet Christmas read.

Love Conquers All: Lanie Perkins Hall never imagined being divorced at thirty. Nor did she imagine falling for an old friend, but when she runs into Azarius Jacobson, she can't deny the attraction. As they begin to spend more time together, Lanie struggles with the fact Azarius keeps his past a secret. What is he hiding? And will she ever be able to get him to open up? Azarius Jacobson has loved Lanie Perkins Hall from the moment he saw her, but issues from his past have left him guarded. Now that he has another chance with her, will he find the courage to share his life with her? Or will his emotional walls create a barrier that will leave him alone once more? Find out in this heartfelt, emotional third book (stand alone) in the Star Lake series.

The Heartbeats Series:

Where It All Began: Sandra Baker thought her life was on the right track until she ended up pregnant. Her boyfriend, not wanting the baby, pushes her to have an abortion. After the procedure, Sandra's life falls apart, and she turns to alcohol. Her relationship ends, and she struggles to find meaning in her life. When she meets Henry Dobbs, a strong Christian man, she begins to wonder if God would accept her. Will she tell Henry her darkest secret? And will she ever be able to forgive herself and find healing? Find out in this emotional love story.

The Power of Prayer: Callie Green thought she had her whole life planned out until her fiance left her at the altar. When her carefully laid plans crumble, she begins to make mistakes at work and engage in uncharacteristic activities. After a mistake nearly costs her her job, she cashes in her honeymoon tickets for some time away. There she meets JD, a charming Christian man who, even though she is not a believer, captures her interest. Before their relationship can deepen, Callie's ex-fiance shows back up in her life and she is forced to choose between Daniel and JD. Who will she choose and how will her choice affect the rest of her life? Find out in this touching novel.

When Hearts Collide: Amanda Adams has always been a Christian, but she's a novice at relationships. When she meets Caleb, her emotions get the best of her and she ignores the sign that something is amiss. Will she find out before it's too late? Jared Masterson is still healing from his girlfriend's strange rejection and disappearance when he meets Amanda. She captivates his heart, but can he save her from making the biggest mistake of her life? A must read for mothers and daughters. Though part of the series and the first of the college spin off series, it is a stand alone book and can be read separately.

A Past Forgiven: Jess Peterson has lived a life of abuse and lost her self worth, but when she is paired with a Christian roommate, she begins to wonder if there is a loving father looking down on her. Her decisions lead her one way, but when she ends up pregnant, she must make some major changes. Chad Michelson is healing from his own past and uses meaningless relationships to hide his pain, but when Jess becomes pregnant, he begins to wonder about the meaning of life. Can he step up and be there for Jess and the baby?

Sweet Billionaires Series:

The Billionaire's Secret: Maxwell Banks was the ultimate player until he found himself caring for a daughter he didn't know he had. Can he change to become the role model she needs? Alyssa Miller hasn't had the best luck with past relationships, so why is she falling for the one man who is sure to break her heart? Though nearly complete opposites, feelings develop, but can Max really change his philandering ways? Or will one mistake seal his fate forever?

A Brush with a Billionaire: Brent just wanted to finish his novel in peace, but when his car breaks down in Sweet Grove, he is forced to deal with a female mechanic and try to get along. Sam thought she had given up on city boys, but when Brent shows up in her shop, she finds herself fighting attraction. Will their stubborn natures keep them apart or can a small town festival bring them together?

The Billionaire's Christmas Miracle: Drew Devonshire is captivated by the woman he meets at a masquerade ball, but who is she? Gwen Rodgers is a teacher, but when she pretends to be her friend and meets Drew at a masquerade ball, her world gets thrown upside down.

The Billionaire's Cowboy Groom: Carrie Bliss finally found the man she wants to marry but there's just one little problem. She's technically still married. Cal Roper hasn't seen her in years but his heart still belongs to his wife. When she returns to town requesting a divorce, can he convince her they belong together?

The Cowboy Billionaire: Coming Soon!

The Lawkeeper Series:
Lawfully Matched: Kate Whidby doesn't want to impose on her newly married brother after their parents die, so she accepts a mail order bride offer in the paper. Little does she know the man she intends to marry has a dark past, sending her fleeing into a neighboring town and into Jesse Jenning's life.

Jesse never wanted to be in law enforcement, but after a band of robbers kills his fiancee, he dons the badge and swears revenge. Will he find his fiancee's killer? And when Kate flies into his life, will he be able to put his painful past behind him in order to love again?

Lawfully Justified: William Cook turns to bounty hunting after losing his wife. When he suffers a life-threatening injury, he is forced to stay in town with an intriguing woman. Emma Stewart has moved back in with her widowed father, the town doctor, but she still longs for a family of her own, so no one is more surprised than she is when she starts to develop feeling for the bounty hunter, who hides his heart of gold behind a rugged exterior. Can Emma offer William a reason to stay? Can William find a way to heal from his broken past to start a future with Emma? Or will a haunting secret take away all the possibilities of this budding romance?

The Scarlet Wedding: William and Emma are planning their wedding, but an outbreak and a return from his past force them to change their plans. Is a happily ever after still in their future?

Lawfully Redeemed: Dani Higgins is a K9 cop looking to make a name for herself, but she finds herself at the mercy of a stranger after an accident. Calvin Phillips just wanted to help his brother, but somehow he ended up in the middle of a police investigation and caring for the woman trying to bring his brother in.

The Still Small Voice Series:

The Still Small Voice: Jordan Wright was searching for something after she gave her son up for adoption. What she found was God, and she began receiving visions. But can she trust Him when he asks her to do something big? Kat Jameson had long been a lukewarm Christian, but when her friend dies and she begins seeing lights, she thinks she is going crazy. Then she meets someone with a message for her. Will she be able to give up control and do what is asked of her?

A Spark in the Darkness coming soon!

Blushing Brides Series:

The Cowboy's Reality Bride: Tyler Hall just wanted to find love, but the women he dated wanted more than his small-town life provided. He gets more than he bargained for when he ends up on a reality dating show and falls for a woman who is not a contestant.

Laney Swann has been running from her past for years, but it takes meeting a man on a reality dating show to make her see there's no need to run.

The Reality Bride's Baby: Laney wants nothing more than a baby, but when she starts feeling dizzy is it pregnancy or something more serious?

The Producer's Unlikely Bride: Justin Miller had given up on love, but when his image needs help, he finds himself needing the aid of a stranger who just happens to be a romance writer. Ava McDermott is waiting for the perfect love, but after agreeing to a fake relationship with Justin, she finds herself falling for real.

Ava's Blessing in Disguise: Five years after marriage, Ava faces a mysterious illness that threatens to ruin her career. Will she find out what it is?

The Soldier's Steadfast Bride: coming soon

The Men of Fire Beach

Fire Games: Cassidy returns home from Who Wants to Marry a Cowboy to find obsessive letters from a fan. The cop assigned to help her wants to get back to his case, but what she sees at a fire may just be the key he's looking for.

Lost Memories and New Beginnings: coming soon

Stand Alones:

Love Renewed: This books is part of the multi author second chance series. When fate reunites high school sweethearts separated by life's choices, can they find a second chance at love at a snowy lodge amid a little mystery?

Her children's early reader chapter book series:

The Wishing Stone #1: Dangerous Dinosaur

The Wishing Stone #2: Dragon Dilemma

The Wishing Stone #3: Mesmerizing Mermaids

The Wishing Stone #4: Pyramid Puzzle

The Wishing Stone Inspirations 1: Mary's Miracle

To see a list of all her books

authorloranahoopes.com
loranahoopes@gmail.com

DISCUSSION QUESTIONS

1. What was your favorite scene in the book? What made it your favorite?

2. Did you have a favorite line in the book? What do you think made it so memorable?

3. Who was your favorite character in the book and why?

4. Where you surprised by any of the events?

5. What do you think would be the hardest part about losing your memory?

6. What did you learn about God from reading this book?

7. How can you use that knowledge in your life from now on?

8. What can you take away from Brody and Tia's relationship?

9. What do you think would make the story even better?

ABOUT THE AUTHOR

Lorana Hoopes is an inspirational author originally from Texas but now living in the PNW with her husband and three children. When not writing, she can be seen kickboxing at the gym, singing, or acting on stage. One day, she hopes to retire from teaching and write full time.